M

My job was to [illegible] from seeing Li. I shif [illegible] her, catching her in the [illegible]section with my shoulder, then slammed her into a wall.

At super speed, I rarely ever hit anything with my bare hand; it's a good way to end up with broken bones. Some speedsters don't care, though; they're so hopped up on adrenaline that they don't feel the pain, and their metabolisms are so high that they heal almost immediately. I didn't feel like testing that theory, and I was in no position to deal with a broken hand, so – while it may not sound gallant – I pistol-whipped Estrella with the gun Li had given me. Then again. And a third time.

Before I could get a fourth turn at bat, she vanished. She had obviously teleported, and my first thought was to check on Li. I'd barely turned my head in that direction when a crushing weight fell on me. Estrella had teleported above me.

Her weight bore me down to the ground, where she cupped my head in her hands, lifted and then smashed it against the concrete floor. I immediately saw stars, as if someone had just put my skull in a car compactor. I tore a page out of her playbook and teleported.

I didn't go far, just a few feet away. I needed to keep her preoccupied so that Li could finish. I raised the gun and fired as she turned in my direction. The light around her body intensified and the bullets seemed to dissolve. At the same time, I became violently ill. I clutched my stomach, doubled over, and threw up.

I was still heaving when Estrella appeared beside me a few seconds later and kneed me in the face.

MUTATION

<u>Kid Sensation Novels</u>
Sensation: A Superhero Novel
Mutation (A Kid Sensation Novel)

<u>The Warden Series</u>
Warden (Book 1: Wendigo Fever)
Warden (Book 2: Lure of the Lamia) (Coming Aug. 2013)

MUTATION
A Kid Sensation Novel

By

Kevin Hardman

MUTATION

This book is a work of fiction contrived by the author, and is not meant to reflect any actual or specific person, place, action, incident or event. Any resemblance to incidents, events, actions, locales or persons, living or dead, factual or fictional, is entirely coincidental.

Copyright © 2013 by Kevin Hardman.

Cover Design by Isikol

This book is published by I&H Recherche Publishing.

All rights reserved, including the right to reproduce this book or portions thereof in any form whatsoever. For information, address I&H Recherche Publishing, P.O. Box 1586, Cypress, TX 77410.

ISBN: 978-1-937666-10-1

Printed in the U.S.A.

MUTATION

ACKNOWLEDGMENTS

I would like to thank the following for their help with this book: GOD, first and foremost (as always) who has continually provided me with strength and guidance; and my family, which has always offered immeasureable encouragement and support.

MUTATION

Chapter 1

Someone once said that invisibility is a power that is really only useful for doing bad things: spying on people; stealing things; playing nasty pranks. Having used my own invisibility to do a couple of those things (I haven't stolen anything yet), I tend to agree. In fact, I was currently using it to spy on a couple who were out on a date. Not just any couple, though - the woman on this date was my mother.

To be frank, I hadn't done anything like this in a long time. Just a few years back, when I was maybe eleven or twelve years old and invisibility was a talent I'd only recently developed, I'd almost made a habit of it. If my mother had a date, I'd wait until they left and then turn invisible. After that, following them was a piece of cake for someone who could fly (as well as phase through walls like a ghost).

Naturally, I didn't think any man was good enough for my mother back then, so I'd do things like trip her date while they were walking. Maybe knock a drink out of his hand so he'd look like a klutz. Or just go for one of the classics and tie his shoelaces together.

Unfortunately, it didn't take long for Mom to put two and two together. (What were the odds of her dating a long string of clumsy oafs?) Afterwards, there came a stern lecture from her and my grandfather, with the result being that I never spied on her during a date again.

Until now.

To be clear, however, I hadn't started out the day intending to tail her. She had already told me earlier in the week that she would be going out, and I really hadn't given it much thought. The truth of the matter is that Mom is exotically beautiful and gets asked out a lot. She could probably have a different date every night of the week if she wanted, but she's very selective - purportedly for my sake, since she's a single mother.

The guy she was going out with was someone I hadn't met before, but that's not unusual. Mom only tends to introduce me to her dates after they've been going out for a while and when there's some type of "potential" to the relationship. In other words, the fact that she wanted me to meet this guy meant something.

His name was Malcolm Schaefer, and I greeted him at the door when he came to pick my mother up. Through the generosity of a friend, we were staying at a spacious house in an upper-middle-class neighborhood. Our own home was in the process of being rebuilt, having been burned to the ground by a fire-wielding supervillain named Incendia. (She had also torched the apartment above our garage that my grandfather lived in.)

Schaefer was about average in height and build, with brown hair, green eyes and a smile that probably set most women's hearts aflutter. Dressed in brown slacks, a white shirt, and a blue blazer, he'd shaken my hand as he came inside, and I'd immediately gotten a weird vibe from him. Being an empath, I normally tune out the emotions of other people, but Schaefer was broadcasting an odd feeling - almost as if he were more excited about me than my mom. I kept my face neutral as my grandfather also came out to meet him, and then we all made small talk until my mother appeared a few seconds later.

Schaefer had commented - as men usually did - on how stunning my mother looked. (I often wondered what they'd think if they knew that part of her appearance came from having an extraterrestrial mother.) Then they had left, but not before he shook my hand again, once more emanating emotions that gave me the distinct impression that something was amiss. Although I knew Mom could probably take care of herself, I wasn't just going to stand idly by when I knew something was wrong.

So there I was, spending my Friday night as a snoop as opposed to being with the girl I was crushing on: Electra. But this was our last free weekend before leaving for school at the Academy, and Electra had some things she needed to take care of. Thus, we wouldn't have been together tonight anyway, although we did have some things planned for tomorrow.

As to Schaefer and my mom, they surprised me by doing the same kinds of things that kids like me do on a date. First, they went to dinner - some middle-of-the-road steakhouse that was too cheap to be considered high class, but too expensive to be construed as low-end. Personally, I was a little miffed that he wasn't pulling out all the stops to impress her: caviar, champagne, the works. Then again, it wasn't their first outing, so maybe he'd already gone through the spend-a-lot-to-impress-your-date phase.

I floated in the air, unseen, above a family of four eating a few tables away. Upon turning invisible, my vision had - as always - reflexively switched over to the infrared, so I saw the world (and everything in it) in varying shades of crimson, scarlet, and the like.

I watched as my mother and Schaefer made small talk, and as she laughed gleefully every now and then at some witticism he made. I wasn't close enough to hear what they were saying, but I wasn't *listening* so much as *feeling.* I had my empathic senses turned up to the max, and one thing came through loud and clear: Schaefer didn't exude the feelings of a man who was on a date with a woman he liked.

Normally, the emotions I pick up from a guy on a date run the gamut from nervousness and trepidation to excitement and titillation. They're dreading the possibility that the date won't go well, elated by the possibility that the girl might like them, etc. Schaefer, however, gave off the vibe of someone stuck in a business meeting.

After dinner, I followed them to the movies. I spent the first hour literally hovering above them in the darkened theater, and then hunger got the better of me. I hadn't eaten anything since this impromptu surveillance had begun. (After all, this was not how I had expected to spend my evening.) Plus, they weren't likely to be going anywhere for a while. That being the case, I phased through the wall and found myself in the hallway leading to the theater.

There were people around, but I didn't think anyone was really looking in my direction so I solidified and became visible. I walked to the concession stand and ordered a couple of candy bars - not the healthiest of meals, but it's catch-as-catch-can when you're on a stakeout. In all honesty, though, I could have just teleported home and wolfed down a sandwich; however, I had essentially snuck into the theater, so I felt I needed to pay for *some*thing (even though movie concession prices are a total rip).

I ate the candy bars out by Schaefer's car. I didn't need to watch my mom for every second of this date, and they'd have to come back to his vehicle to leave. He drove a limited-edition black Mercedes Benz. Leaning over, I phased through the driver's window and took a peek inside. The car contained a high-end instrument panel, as well as an impressive entertainment console. There was GPS, satellite music, a DVD screen. Like Schaefer himself, the car seemed too smooth, too slick, and as I phased back out of the vehicle I fought a weird, juvenile compulsion to smear chocolate on the driver's side door handle.

While waiting for the movie to end, I spent the next hour lying, invisible, on the roof of the Benz, looking up at the stars. There's something about staring at the nighttime sky that just relaxes me. It always gives me a sense of serenity.

At long last, I heard my mother and her date approaching, discussing the merits of the movie they'd seen. I silently floated up from the roof of the car into the air.

****

I found myself somewhat relieved that Schaefer drove my mother straight home after the movie. Thankfully, she didn't invite him in for a nightcap; their goodbyes were said at the door, and punctuated by a short kiss on the lips. Still invisible, I phased through the car door and into the back seat of his vehicle.

Schaefer got back into the car and began driving. After a few minutes, he pressed a button on the entertainment console, and I heard the distinct drone of a telephone dial tone. Apparently there was a phone system built into the car as well.

"Call Nighthawk," Schaefer said.

MUTATION

The chimes of numbers being dialed on a touch-tone phone sounded, followed by a number of odd clicks. Presumably, the number that Schaefer had dialed was being filtered through various channels in order to minimize the possibility of the call being traced. I sat up, listening intently.

After a few seconds there was an odd, hollow ringing. The phone was answered almost immediately. However, neither Schaefer nor the person on the other end said anything.

"Confirmed," a male voice on the other end finally said after a lengthy silence. "Line is clear."

"This is Walker, calling in to report." Schaefer said. "Identification number two-seven-alpha-psi-nine."

"Voice ID and number confirmed. You are free to report."

"Contact with target finally established," Schaefer stated, and I felt the same emotional discharge from him that I'd picked up on earlier when he shook my hand. "Requesting instructions regarding Phase Two."

"Acknowledged. Pick-up point for Phase Two instructions will be delivered tomorrow."

"Understood." With that, Schaefer (or Walker, whatever his name was) hit another button on the console, disconnecting the call.

In the back seat, I was trying to make sense of what I had heard. Schaefer/Walker had mentioned "finally" making contact. It was unlikely that he meant my mother (since he already knew her), and based on what I'd picked up from him emotionally, there was little doubt that I was the target in his crosshairs. Basically, this clown was just using Mom to get close to me, which really got

6

me fuming. But I still had more questions than answers: who was he working with? What did they want with me?

Whoever they were, it was obviously someone who knew that I was Kid Sensation. No one who knew me as Jim Carrow would find me interesting. If asked, they'd probably describe me as a quiet kid, not a troublemaker but a bit of a loner.

For a second, I debated prying the info out of Schaefer/Walker. As a telepath, I can - technically - read minds, but it's not something I do on a regular basis. Long story short, going deep into other people's brains makes me physically ill. It's as if the other person's mind is the house of a hoarder, fill with all kinds of garbage, trash, filth, and debris. It's completely unsanitary.

On the flip side, however, I can broadcast my thoughts to people – and pick up surface thoughts and what they willingly want to share – with ease when I want. For me, that's akin to standing outside the hoarder's house and communicating with them through an open window. In other words, I don't get exposed to the unhealthy conditions in their mind that way.

The sudden deceleration of the car brought me back to myself. While I had been busy internally debating whether to try to read his mind, Schaefer/Walker had driven into an underground garage and was parking the car. A quick glance around revealed a sign that indicated that we were in the parking area for guests of a posh five-star hotel. (And he couldn't treat Mom to an expensive dinner?)

Schaefer was getting out of the car, so I made the decision to just try the direct approach. I teleported behind him and became visible as he was shutting the door to his car.

"Boo," I said as he turned around.

Startled, Schaefer/Walker took a step back, at the same time seeming to reach behind him for something. However, he stopped in mid-motion and looked closely at me.

"Jim?" He stared at me in open surprise. "What are you doing here?"

"I figured we needed to talk," I answered.

"Talk? About what?"

"Why don't we start with Nighthawk and go from there."

"I see," he said, eyes narrowing. "But why don't we discuss this up in my suite?" He walked past me without waiting for a response, heading towards the hotel elevator. I fell in step behind him, ruminating on the fact that he had a *suite* in a swanky hotel, but took the cheap route on his date with my mother.

"Ahh…" he muttered as he began patting his pockets. "This elevator requires a room key to operate. Security, you know."

I was only half paying attention when he suddenly swung around with some kind of weapon in his hand. It bore an odd resemblance to a gun, but instead of a barrel, it had some metal studs on the end.

Some kind of stun gun, I thought as he fired. I shifted into super speed, and the world slowed down around me. I watched the probes approach and then sidestepped them. I slowed back down to normal speed.

"Bad move, dude," I said as I teleported the weapon from his hand and into mine.

MUTATION

Chapter 2

I will say one thing for Schaefer (Walker was apparently a code name), he was indeed well-trained. Of course, I had never tried to extract information from anybody before, so it could have been my lack of experience that made him seem so formidable. Still, I like to think that I did more than just give it the old college try.

He hadn't talked after I'd taken the stun gun from him and asked nicely. He still refused to say a word when I teleported him to a frosty mountain peak where a blizzard was blowing. He also continued showing steely resistance after I took him to a height of a thousand feet and let him drop. Nothing I tried seemed to work, and I had almost resolved to try reading his mind when I remembered a trick my grandfather had taught me.

I telepathically parked myself right outside his mental house and - peeking in through a "window" - asked him, "What are you most afraid of?"

Needless to say, he didn't respond verbally, but an image flashed through his brain and I was inside just enough to get a glimpse of it. I smiled to myself, and then teleported us to the shark tank at the city's aquarium.

We were actually in the observation room, with its huge glass walls that let you see inside the various fish habitats. A huge great white - at least fifteen feet long - swam by a second after we appeared, its mouth open and full of monstrous teeth. Schaefer took one look and went white as a sheet. (He hadn't even looked this white after I'd teleported him out of that blizzard.)

"No," he murmured. "You can't…"

I didn't feel like arguing. I popped him into the shark tank.

It was almost comical. As he had been in the middle of saying something, Schaefer appeared in the tank with his mouth open and working. His eyes suddenly bulged, not just from having water suddenly gushing into his lungs, but also from the sight of a massive three-ton image of appetite and teeth suddenly heading in his direction.

From the way his mouth moved, I imagine he was trying to scream as the shark closed in on him. The huge mouth opened, then clamped down...

...on nothing.

I had phased Schaefer, making him insubstantial so that the shark passed through him as if he were a ghost.

I teleported him back out of the shark habitat. He collapsed to the ground, completely soaked and retching uncontrollably. The whole ordeal had lasted less than ten seconds, but it was another five minutes before he coughed up all of the water in his lungs and was able to speak. And at that point, he was ready to tell me everything.

MUTATION

Chapter 3

The Men in Black showed up the next day around noon. Frankly speaking, I had expected them earlier, but maybe they got caught in traffic.

My mother had just left to run some errands, leaving me and my grandfather playing video games. The old man was crushing me in NCAA Football when he suddenly sighed in annoyance and hit the pause button.

"Get the door," he said. "We've got company."

Gramps is psychic (a universal term for anyone with mental powers), and was once the most powerful telepath on the planet. He had been retired for a while now, but his abilities had only mildly diminished from his days as an active superhero.

I went to the door and opened it just as the MIBs were preparing to knock. Correction: I opened it just as a man in a pinstriped gray suit was about to knock; however, MIBs formed a tight semi-circle around him - one on each side and two behind. They were dressed in accordance with urban legend - black suits, white shirts, black ties, and sunglasses. (Obviously these guys believe their own press.)

Knuckles poised to rap on the door, the man in the gray suit looked a little surprised when I opened it. He appeared to be in his early sixties, with iron-gray hair that he wore combed back. He gave me a smile that didn't quite reach his cold, gray eyes and extended a hand towards me.

"You must be Jim," he said, pumping my hand as we shook. He had a strength that belied his age, and I felt an emotional intensity deeply embedded within him.

There was some driving force in this man, but I didn't quite know what it was.

"It's okay to call you 'Jim,' right?" he asked, as I disengaged my hand from his. "Or do you prefer 'Kid Sensation'?"

"Jim's fine," I responded, keeping my face and voice neutral. After my conversation with Schaefer last night, it wasn't any surprise that they knew who I was. I kept my position in the doorway, my body language making it clear that they weren't invited in. "And you are…?"

"Gray," my grandfather said from the interior of the house behind me. "That's Mr. Gray. Go ahead and let them in."

I stepped aside and Gray entered, followed by the MIBs, who fanned out and took up strategic locations around our living room. One stayed by the door. Another stepped to the walkway between the living room and kitchen. The third stood by the stairs and the fourth just took a position in a corner of the room whereby he could see everything and everyone.

Gray went straight to my grandfather and shook his hand. "Good to see you, John."

My grandfather returned the handshake without comment. He motioned to a nearby recliner, which Gray plopped down into. My grandfather and I sat back down on the sofa in the positions we'd previously held while playing the video game.

"So what's it been, John - forty years?" Gray asked.

"No," Gramps answered. "Forty years ago is when you crashed my wedding. It's been more like thirty-five, but it feels like yesterday."

Gray chuckled. "Look, I think we both know I was just doing my job. I wasn't trying to harass you."

"Really? My wife and I saw it differently."

"Wait a minute," I interjected. The conversation had taken a decidedly personal turn: they were talking about my grandmother. "Gramps, who is this guy?"

"Mr. Gray here runs the MIB organization, and their primary focus is extraterrestrials."

"Huh?" I was really just being facetious when I'd called them that earlier. "There really is an MIB organization?"

"Actually, our official name is classified," Gray said. "But 'MIB' works for us."

I was somewhat surprised. "So even your agency name is classified?"

Gray responded with an acquiescent shrug.

Gramps grunted in annoyance. "Don't get too chummy with him, Jim. Gray here made me and your grandmother his own pet project from the time we were engaged up until the moment she left."

"What did you expect?" Gray demanded. "You married an *alien*, John. Nobody knew anything about her, where she came from, what her intentions truly were, and suddenly she's got access to the most powerful telepath on the planet! A man who can read anyone's mind - who can find out about our latest weapons technology, or dig nuclear launch codes out of the president's brain!"

My grandmother, Indigo, was an alien princess from a distant planet. Mom had been an infant when her mother had been compelled to return to her homeworld, leaving my grandfather to raise their daughter on his own. They'd had enough problems to deal with at the time – him with his dusky complexion and her with skin like

13

porcelain. It had never occurred to me that they were also being hassled by the government.

"And did any of that ever happen?" My grandfather asked.

"No," Gray admitted, smiling. "No, it did not. In fact, she became a superhero and a member of the Alpha League. But of course, you already know all this."

"Yes, but thanks for the history lesson," Gramps said. "Anyway, to what do we owe the pleasure?"

Gray's face darkened a bit before he replied. "I'm afraid it's serious, John. Your boy here assaulted a federal officer last night."

I felt a slight mental probe from my grandfather. <???>

<Later,> I responded. I hadn't told him about spying on my mother's date and the whole thing with Schaefer, but I'd known that I would have to, eventually.

"Jim, don't say a word," my grandfather cautioned, his expression never changing. It struck me as sound advice, so I kept my mouth shut.

"He doesn't have to say anything," Gray quipped. "We have a sworn statement from the agent involved."

"Did he identify himself as a federal agent?"

"He flashed his badge," Gray answered, which was true. After our sojourn to the blizzard-whipped mountain peak, Schaefer had pulled a little gold shield from his pocket and declared himself to be with some agency or other. I was so intent on getting usable info from him that I hadn't even paid attention to the name of the organization he said he worked for. Using telekinesis, I had yanked the shield from his hand and then crumpled it like a wad of paper.

"Well, if he works for you, Gray, then anything dealing with Jim is outside his scope of authority. Your jurisdiction is limited to extraterrestrials, so he couldn't have been acting in an official capacity."

"Actually, your grandson falls dead center into my wheelhouse."

My grandfather scoffed. "You're crazy. Jim's not an alien of any sort. He was born on *this* planet, in a local hospital in fact, which makes him a citizen of this country, just like you and me."

Gray turned to me. "John Indigo Morrison Carrow. Also known as Jim Carrow. Also known as Kid Sensation. Born sixteen years ago to Geneva Carrow – herself the natural daughter of the alien known as Indigo – and the alien super known as Alpha Prime."

I kept all of the emotion out of my face as he spoke. They had clearly done their homework; very few people knew that I was the son of Alpha Prime, the world's greatest superhero.

Turning his gaze back to my grandfather, Gray stated, "With three-fourths of his physiology being alien, I would argue that my authority definitely extends to him."

"Except your math is wrong," I chimed in, ignoring the concerned glance Gramps gave me. "My father's from an alternate dimension, not an alien world. He's as human as anybody else – just more powerful."

"Fine, then," Gray countered. "You're one-fourth extra*terrestrial*, two-fourths extra-*dimensional*. Doesn't change the fact that, based on bloodlines, our planet has the weakest claim on your loyalties."

Gramps was frowning. "You're construing loyalty based on genetics? That's not just outside the extent of your commission, it's completely absurd."

Gray simply shook his head. "You've been out of the game a long time, John. Things have changed."

"Like what?"

"Like the fact that my agency's authority and jurisdiction has been expanded exponentially. Ever since the V'lgrath invasion a few years ago, a lot of people have become extremely concerned with what might gently be described as 'alien infestation'."

"What the hell does that mean?"

"It means that the world is suddenly quite keenly aware of illegal aliens living here – and I'm not talking about people slipping across borders. I'm talking about beings from other worlds, sneaking onto the planet with powers, abilities, and technology that we know nothing about and which could pose a significant harm to terrestrial life."

"Jim's no threat, and you know it. You've been watching him his whole life, just like you did his mother."

Gray raised an eyebrow slightly in surprise.

Gramps went on. "What, you think I didn't know? You might not have shown your face in over three decades, but you didn't think I could feel you guys out there? Watching my daughter as she grew up? Spying on her friends? Noting the birth of my grandson? Keeping tabs on him his whole life?"

I had to fight to keep my mouth from dropping open. These people had had me under a microscope since the day I was born?

"All true," Gray admitted, "but out of respect for you, John, and the service you've done for your country –

and your world – we tried to give you a reasonable amount of privacy. We never bugged your phone, your home, anything like that. We kept a respectful distance."

"Until now," I said. With that, I opened up a mental link with my grandfather and shared with him my escapades from the night before.

Communication between two telepaths – especially those that share a bond, like kinship – is often a high-speed affair. It's beyond just conveying words; it's also images, emotions, concepts, and more. Basically, it only took a few seconds for me to bring him up to speed on what had happened. However, instead of the explosive anger I thought would result, I felt only mild vexation from him.

"If you're talking about sending agents to date your mother," Gray noted, "let me just say that that is a relatively new development. As I said earlier, our jurisdiction has increased, so we've started taking additional steps to encompass our expanded mission. In essence, we've got carte blanche to do whatever we want on a global scale."

Gramps frowned. "So what does that mean as far as Jim is concerned?"

Gray shrugged. "It depends on how he's perceived. If we decide that he's a threat, we could strip him of his citizenship and deport him."

My grandfather laughed. "What, kick him out of the country? Go ahead. You seem to forget that as Kid Sensation, he saved the world just a few weeks ago; his role in it may not be public knowledge, but enough people in the right circles know. He'll have a dozen countries lined up to offer him residence - especially if word of it gets leaked to the press."

Gray made a tsking sound. "You weren't listening, John. Our authority is global now, so I'm not talking about stripping him of *national* citizenship."

My grandfather's eyes went wide, and I felt anger starting to boil in him as the full implications of what Gray was saying sank in. I'm pretty sure I looked to be in shock myself.

"Offworld? You'd deport him off the planet? Where would he go?"

"Not my problem," Gray said indifferently. "And as to the media, we can suppress pretty much any story we want, or spin it in a light that's favorable to us."

Gray lean forward conspiratorially. "But let's not put the cart before the horse. I'm talking about things that could *possibly* happen if Jim here is believed to be a threat. However, if he were to exhibit some token of loyalty, something to let us know whose side he was on…"

"Cut to the chase, Gray," Gramps said. "What do you really want?"

Gray cleared his throat before speaking. "I want your grandson to work for us."

Chapter 4

"What?" I asked incredulously.

"It's simple enough," Gray said. "You're going to be attending the Academy in-residence, learning what it means to be a superhero along with hundreds of other students. It may come as a surprise, but it's the single largest gathering of superpowered beings that we know of."

"It's a bunch of kids!" I shouted. "A bunch of teenagers, all still in high school. That's all the Academy is: a big high school for teen supers."

"Some of whom are incredibly powerful," Gray added. "Like yourself. The whole world saw how you singlehandedly took down the Alpha League following your tryout."

I frowned and shamefully lowered my head. Two years earlier, during the ceremony to induct me as a Teen Super with the Alpha League, an altercation with another teen had erupted into a full-scale battle with me on one side and a bunch of superheroes on the other. In retrospect, no one really blamed me for what happened, but the incident was a major embarrassment for everyone involved - especially since it was all caught on tape.

"Are you trying to say that supers - even *terrestrial* supers - now fall under your purview?" Gramps asked.

"I'm saying that whatever I decide is under my purview is what's under my purview," Gray smirked. "Think of me as a modern-day J. Edgar Hoover, but without the same limitations on authority. So if I decide it's supers, then it's supers."

That sounded bad - on several levels.

"Since when?" my grandfather demanded.

"Since a bunch of so-called superheroes went rogue and tried to take over the world!"

"First of all, those were super teens, not full-fledged capes," Gramps retorted. "Number two, Jim here is the reason they failed. You should be giving him a medal, not harassing him."

Gray snorted dismissively. "Well, before you get too generous with bestowing glory on your grandson, bear in mind that Paramount, the leader of that rogue group, was his brother."

"Uh, half-brother," I corrected. "And we never had any familial interaction."

"Doesn't matter," Gray said. "You're guilty by association."

I raised my hands in exasperation. "How can I be guilty by association regarding someone I never associated with? Paramount didn't even know we were related!"

"So says you," Gray countered. "But back to the subject at hand - the Academy. As you stated, Jim, the majority of the population there is a bunch of kids. Teens like yourself. Young, immature to some extent, and probably very impressionable."

"That's teens everywhere," I said.

"True," Gray admitted, "but the teens at most high schools don't pack enough combined firepower to destroy the planet ten times over. And right now, we don't have a firm idea of what they're being taught."

"Huh?" My grandfather interjected. "Are you telling me that you can't get information about what goes on at the Academy? That's a crock!"

"We get reports, true enough," Gray stated. "But we've got no way to verify their accuracy. What do we

20

really know about what those kids are being taught? What are they learning about patriotism? Love of country? Loyalty to their home planet? Paramount's entire clique consisted of people at that school, so we need better intel on what's going on there."

"So that's how it happened," Gramps said. "This increase in power you've been given - including authority over supers - is a direct result of that incident with Paramount."

"Incident" seemed too mild a word for it. Led by Paramount, a group of super teens had joined forces with a half-dozen of the worst supervillains on the planet. We managed to foil their plans, but it kind of left the superhero community with a black eye from a public relations standpoint.

"You always were a smart one, John," Gray said in acquiescence. "But the machinery to make the changes was already in the works. That thing with Paramount just kind of greased the wheels, made it all happen quicker."

My grandfather was clearly unimpressed. "So now, instead of just bullying extraterrestrials, you also get to strong-arm kids like my grandson."

"I'm not trying to muscle anybody. I'm just asking young Jim here to show us where his loyalties lie by giving us a pair of eyes on the ground at the Academy."

"You mean be a spy," I said. Gray just shrugged noncommittally. "What if I don't want to do it?"

"Then, after last night's assault on Schaefer, I may have to declare you a danger and consider my options," Gray stated sternly. "But I'm a reasonable man. You don't leave for the Academy for another couple of days. I'll give you until then to think it over."

MUTATION

He got up to leave, and the MIBs moved in unison to flank him as before. They had been so still and silent during our conversation that I'd almost forgotten they were there.

As they were walking out the door, Gray stopped and turned to me.

"Just so we're clear, I'll be expecting your answer before you depart." He handed me a card made of heavy white stock. There was nothing but a phone number on it in a large, raised font. "It would be a mistake to take off for the Academy without talking to me first."

And with that, they were gone.

Chapter 5

"You knew," I said to my grandfather after Gray and his entourage had left. "You knew that Schaefer was a phony."

My grandfather just shrugged. "How'd you figure that out?"

"You. Your reactions. Normally, you blow your stack regarding anything that's a threat to me or Mom. But when I told you about Schaefer, you were just annoyed."

"I was more irritated by the fact that you'd found out about it than the act itself."

"Does Mom know?"

"Of course."

I should have guessed as much. She doesn't put it on display very often, but Mom's a powerful telepath in her own right. There was even a time when she had ventured to become a superhero herself, but then I came along and derailed those plans before they'd come anywhere close to fruition.

"If she knew, then why did she go out with him?"

"To keep Gray and his crew off-guard," Gramps responded. "Did you think this was the first time they tried to get close to us? To *you*? If she continually turned down dates from all their agents, they would have figured out we were on to them. This way, we avoided suspicion."

"Until I screwed it up." I was aghast at what I'd done. It was like I'd blown someone's cover on a secret mission. Even worse, I'd done it for almost no reason, because Schaefer hadn't really known anything. He'd been aware that I was a super, and his initial assignment was to date Mom in order to get close to me. Beyond that, however, his knowledge was severely limited. (He didn't even know who his contact, "Nighthawk," actually was.) Apparently all of the mission-critical information was to be delivered to him later - presumably as part of the "Phase Two" I'd heard mentioned.

"Don't beat yourself up about it," Gramps said with a smile. "It's pretty clear they were planning to approach you soon anyway. You just pushed up their timetable."

"So now what?"

"Now nothing. You just keep doing what you've been doing."

"What about Gray's offer?"

"You mean his ultimatum? That's up to you. You're old enough to start making these decisions for yourself. But if you're asking my advice, Gray's considered a necessary evil by the powers that be, but he's the last person you want to crawl into bed with."

****

After our conversation about Gray, Gramps took me for a driving lesson. A few weeks earlier, I had been greatly ashamed when – after arranging to take a girl on a date – it came to light that I didn't know how to drive. (In my defense, being a teleporter and a speedster means that a car is a superfluous item.) Shortly thereafter, I had made daily driving lessons a high priority. I had made a lot of progress, but was not quite proficient enough to get a license.

After the lesson ended, I teleported to an Alpha League safe house for my date with Electra. The League's headquarters had suffered extensive damage when Paramount went off the reservation. Much of it had been repaired, but Mouse – the *de facto* head of the Alpha League – had decided to use the reconstruction to incorporate several significant changes.

"We're rebuilding anyway," he'd said. "Why not use the opportunity to make some meaningful improvements?"

What those improvements were exactly had yet to be made common knowledge, but the upshot of it all was that the League was operating out of various safe houses for the moment. Aside from Mouse's lab, League HQ was not yet fully functional.

The safe house where I was meeting Electra was a boarded-up tenement in one of the worst parts of town. It was flanked on one side by a notorious crackhouse, and on the other by a burned-out shell of a building that basically served as housing for a large number of homeless people.

To the outside world, the safe house appeared deserted, but it was definitely one of those instances where you shouldn't judge a book by its cover. The interior was decidedly high-end in terms of layout, facilities, accommodations, and capabilities. By way of example, the exterior doors on the ground floor appeared to be made of wood, but were actually reinforced steel encased in a wooden shell. Many a crackhead had dislocated a shoulder or broken a toe trying to batter or kick their way in. (And even if they had managed to get inside, the doorways were always guarded.)

There were two primary points of ingress and egress: an unboarded door under the front stoop that led to the basement, and the roof. I appeared in front of the basement door, as I always did, because it was situated in such a manner that no one could see me as I teleported in.

I stood there silently while unseen equipment scanned my biometrics, trying to determine if entry was authorized. After about ten seconds, there was a soft click and the door cracked open. I stepped inside and the door closed automatically behind me. I was now in a small cube-shaped room, three of the walls of which were made of bulletproof glass. Outside the room stood three guards – one to my left, one to my right, and one directly in front of me. Despite the bulletproof glass, the two on the sides of the room held their weapons, semi-automatic assault rifles, at the ready (never mind the fact that I – in my loafers, khakis, golf shirt, and sports coat – hardly appeared threatening). The third stood at a control panel and, via a two-way comm system, asked me a series of questions that verified my identity.

Being a shapeshifter, my abilities had required the League to adopt some additional security measures. Fingerprints, retinal patterns, and voice-recognition software weren't all that effective when dealing with someone who could change their appearance and voice at will. In those circumstances, it paid to go old-school and just do a run-of-the-mill Q&A.

I passed the security check with flying colors, at which point a seam appeared in the glass in front of me. It expanded, taking on the shape of a large vertically-standing rectangle, which then slid up into the ceiling, thereby providing an exit. Had I failed the security check, two portholes would have appeared on the sides of the glass chamber, allowing the guards there to insert the barrels of their guns and fire at will.

MUTATION

I stepped out of the little glass room and towards the guard at the control panel. To the left of where he was stationed was a set of elevator doors, which opened with a slight musical *ding*. I stepped inside and pressed the button for the fifth floor, which was where I was meeting Electra.

The fifth floor was a common area/break room, offering food and drinks as well as various popular games such as table tennis. One thing I had quickly noticed upon spending more time with the Alpha League was that they tended to spend liberally when it came to recreation; I had yet to visit one of their facilities that did not have swimming pools, video games, pool tables, or the like. However, being a superhero is clearly a stressful and dangerous occupation, so I didn't begrudge them these small perks.

The break room here fell in line with my expectations, but was fairly deserted. League members were operating out of several safe houses around town, and those who weren't out on missions were probably over at HQ, helping with reconstruction. Thus, there were only about a half-dozen super teens scattered around the room, a couple of whom looked my way and waved. Just a few weeks ago I had practically been mobbed by a group of super teens at League HQ after Mouse introduced me to them as the infamous Kid Sensation. Now, just a few weeks later, the novelty of my presence had apparently worn off.

Speaking of Mouse, however, I was surprised to see him sitting at a nearby table, talking to Vixen. Normally, if he wasn't off on a mission, he was hard at work in his lab. He waved me over.

"Have a seat," he said as I approached. I pulled up a chair and sat down.

Despite his moniker, Mouse wasn't some tiny pipsqueak. He was big – six-three or so – with an impressive (but not over-muscled) physique. As always, he was clean-shaven, with jet-black hair and clear blue eyes. All in all, he would have been the consummate matinee idol a few decades ago, and as it was, a lot of the females among the super teens had mad crushes on him.

Vixen was a Siren, so by definition she was a complete stunner. The League's trademark black-and-gold uniform, which both she and Mouse wore, emphasized the fact that she was the female form perfected, and with luxurious red hair and clear, flawless skin. She'd never really done anything untoward with respect to me, but she was one of the few supers I usually kept my guard up around. As a Siren, she was also empathic, with the power to manipulate the opposite sex, and as an empath myself, I generally found myself remaining on edge in her presence.

"So, how's everything going?" Mouse asked.

"Great until I got here," I said. "You guys couldn't find an unoccupied landfill to operate out of?"

"Funny," Mouse responded without conviction. "The purpose of a safe house is to provide a secure location where you'll be safe from actual and potential danger, preferably a place where your enemies won't think to look for you."

"And no one will think to look for the world's premiere superhero team at Crack Market Central."

"No, they won't," Mouse said, "and it's not that bad."

"Easy for you to say," Vixen interjected, "since you get to spend all of your time back at HQ in your lab."

"Don't take his side," Mouse said, shaking his head. "He already thinks he's the greatest thing since sliced bread. I don't need him thinking he's right all the time."

The conversation then devolved into a little debate between the two of them. It wasn't common knowledge, but Vixen and Mouse were a couple. I hadn't seen any overt displays of affection between them, but I had picked up on the emotions they exuded in each other's presence. Plus, these little verbal sparring matches between them made it seem that they were closer than mere colleagues or co-workers.

"Anyway," Mouse finally said, turning back to me, "how are things *really* going?"

"Pretty well," I said. "A little slow for the most part."

Mouse chuckled. "Yeah. Regular life seems kind of dull after you've saved the world. Just wait until you've done it a dozen times, then you'll really get jaded."

"Don't pay any attention to him," Vixen interjected. "He's just grumpy because the reconstruction isn't taking place as fast as he'd like – even though his lab was the first thing that got fixed."

"Which begs the question," I said. "Why are you here?"

"To talk to you. About the Academy."

Most superhero teams had a teen affiliate – part of the Teen Development League. I was with the Alpha League's teen group, and each of us was assigned a League member as a mentor. Mouse was mine, and part of his job was to make sure I was ready for living in-residence at the Academy.

I glanced at my watch. 1:33 p.m. Ordinarily I'm keen to hear almost anything Mouse has to say, but we were really operating on a tight time schedule today.

Mouse saw the look of concern on my face. "Relax," he said. "I know all about your date with Electra. This won't take long. Besides, if you know anything at all about women, you know that she's going to be late anyway."

That earned him a glare from Vixen, which he subtly ignored.

"It's not a problem," I stated nonchalantly. "Go ahead."

"Great. The main thing is, we got your test scores back. You qualify for all advanced courses, so congrats." He slapped me on the back for emphasis.

The week prior, I'd had to take a number of tests to determine where I should be placed academically. At sixteen, I would have been a junior in a normal high school, but at the Academy, the courses you take aren't strictly age-based. A lot of it has to do with current knowledge, IQ, and potential.

I groaned audibly and rolled my eyes. I liked school and had always done well as a student, but I'd heard that you had to work your butt off just to keep up in the *regular* classes at the Academy. The workload in the advanced courses was the stuff of urban legends.

"It's not as bad as all that," Mouse noted sympathetically. "It's not some medieval torture, despite what you may have heard. It's designed to help you reach your full potential."

When I didn't respond, he went on. "Look, Jim, you're an amazing kid. You've got probably the greatest power set of anybody who ever lived, and you're still young, still developing new abilities. But on top of that, you've got a remarkable brain, and you showed it in that conflict a few weeks back. Oddly enough, though, that's the area where you have the most untapped potential, and that's what I want to focus on developing. You already have a firm grip on your powers, but combine that with what I know you can do upstairs" – he tapped his temple for emphasis – "and then you'll really be worthy of the name 'Kid Sensation' and no one will be able to hold a candle to you."

"Fine," I muttered in exasperation. "But if I flunk these courses, it's on your head."

Mouse smiled at that. "So be it. Now, there's just one other thing…" He turned towards Vixen.

Vixen just stared at him blankly for a second, and then it hit her. "Oh. Guy talk. Well, excu-u-u-use me." She stood up in something of a huff, then stalked from the room.

"Alpha Prime," Mouse said, turning back to me. "You need to talk to him before you leave for the Academy."

I cringed on the inside. Mouse was one of the few people outside my family (and apparently the MIBs) who knew that Alpha Prime was my father. However, he'd never really been part of my life.

"I *do* speak to him," I said. "I've bumped into him a couple of times over the past few weeks – here and at HQ – and I'm always courteous."

"I'm not talking about being courteous. I'm talking about a real father-son talk."

31

"We've had one. Basically, he walked out of my life before I was even born and never looked back."

"He did that to protect you. You know that."

"Oh? The way he protected his other son? See, he didn't have any problem showcasing Paramount to the world as his child. But me – he didn't reach out to me until his number-one son went bonkers and killed a bunch of people. That's when he suddenly realized that maybe there's some joy in having a child who *isn't* a homicidal maniac."

"That's completely unfair and you know it. Come on, Jim. You're better than that. You can't expect him to do all the heavy lifting."

"He's the world's greatest superhero," I said in exasperation. "Who better to do the heavy lifting?"

Mouse just cocked his head to the side and stared at me.

"Fine," I mumbled after a few seconds. "I promised my mother a while back that I'd try with him, so I'll give it a little more effort."

"Sounds good."

At that moment, Electra came into the room. She smiled when she saw me and headed in our direction.

Her shoulder-length hair, dark and straight, had obviously been trimmed quite recently. As usual, she wore little makeup or jewelry; she had a natural beauty that cosmetics tended to hamper, so she rarely utilized them (except for a shade of red lipstick that she had somehow figured out I liked seeing on her). In terms of clothes, she wore a pair of sandals, jeans, and a flutter-sleeved top.

I stood up as she got close, and found myself returning her infectious smile.

"Hey you," she said, taking my hand. "Ready to go?"

"Yeah," I said. I turned to Mouse and held out my hand. "Later."

"Don't forget what we talked about," he said as he shook my hand. "By the way, where are you guys going?"

Electra grinned. "He won't tell me. It's a surprise."

"Well, don't have her out too late," stressed a voice behind me. I glanced around and saw Vixen, who apparently had returned just in time to see us off. "I'd hate to have to come after you."

She was only half-joking, I knew. Electra was an orphan, and had been raised with the entire Alpha League as her guardian. I'm not sure any one person in particular saw themselves in the parental role, but quite a few of them – especially the younger ones like Vixen and Mouse, who had only been in the League a few years – looked upon her as a little sister (which might have been even worse). Plus, Electra and I were both part of Alpha League's group of teen supers. In short, there were a million ways this relationship could go wrong and have nasty repercussions.

We said our goodbyes and I was about to teleport us out of there (I had something special planned) when Vixen spoke up again.

"Electra, do you mind if I borrow your boyfriend for a second before you guys take off?" she asked.

I felt my cheeks turning red. What Electra and I had was still pretty new, and as such we hadn't put any labels on it yet. Thus, I was about to protest and say that I wasn't her boyfriend when Electra cut me off.

"That's fine," she answered. "I want to ask Mouse something anyway."

With that, Vixen dragged me over to a far corner of the room.

"I need you to do me a favor," she said.

"Sure," I said, nodding.

"I need for you to do well in your classes at the Academy."

"Okay," I said, slightly confused. "But I was planning to do my best anyway."

"Not your best," she said. "I need you to *excel*."

I frowned. "I'm not following you."

She sighed and lowered her head in thought for a moment. "How much do you know about Sirens?"

I shrugged. "About the same as everyone, I suppose. Beautiful. Empathic. Able to manipulate the opposite sex."

"Did you know that we bond for life? With a mate?"

"No," I said, shaking my head. "I've never heard that before. My understanding is that you're all slu–...uh, flirts."

"It has to be the right male," she said, ignoring my last comment. She glanced in Mouse's direction, where he was talking to Electra. "But when we meet him, something's triggered in our DNA. We have to be with him and only him."

"And Mouse is that guy for you?" I asked. She nodded. "But what does that have to do with me?"

She turned her attention back to me. "With most guys, bonding with a Siren isn't an issue. They can't get enough of us. But, as you've probably figured out by now, Mouse isn't most men."

I thought for a second. "So, you're saying that the power that Sirens usually have over men doesn't work on Mouse?"

"Not to the same degree."

"I still don't understand how it relates to me and my studies."

She let out an exasperated sigh. "Mouse needs someone he can talk to."

"Isn't that where you come in? I thought most women wanted their guys to talk to them."

"No, I'm not talking about normal everyday stuff. He needs someone he can talk to about all the high-level, scientific crap that's always running through his brain. According to the tests, you've got a genius-level IQ. Ergo, you're elected."

I frowned at that. Not so much that I had tested as having a high IQ – I'd been tested before – but because Vixen was essentially asking me to become Mouse's intellectual peer.

"That's a tall order," I said. "There's got to be someone else who can pick up the slack."

"There are, but let me share something with you: when he saw your scores, he was super-excited. He may have acted nonchalantly here today, but he couldn't stop raving about how great it was going to be to work with you on some of his projects. So I need you to go to the Academy, study your butt off, and come back here a complete whiz in every subject. Because if you don't…"

She looked away, and her lip sort of trembled. I felt odd emotions starting to flow from her - distress and anguish, rooted in loss.

"You're afraid," I said in sudden comprehension. "You think that he's going to get bored around here. Get bored intellectually and leave."

She didn't say anything, just gave an almost imperceptible nod.

"Okay," I said, nodding in agreement. "I'll give it my all."

She suddenly looked up with a smile, then gave me a hug and a kiss on the cheek. As I left with Electra, I couldn't help but wonder if Vixen had somehow just used her power to manipulate *me*.

MUTATION

Chapter 6

I had promised Electra a surprise for our date, so I made her close her eyes when I teleported us. When she opened them, I could see that she was a little disappointed. We were in a long, wide building with high ceilings. Exquisite paintings hung on the walls.

"A museum?" she asked, looking around. "What's so special about this?"

I smiled and just pointed behind her, where a large group of people were amassed around a single painting, jostling each other and snapping pictures.

"What is that?" Electra asked as she started moving towards the crowd. "What are they all looking at?"

"*La Joconde*," I said, taking off my sports coat. Telescoping my vision, I was able to see the portrait easily, but Electra still needed to get closer.

She kept moving forward, squinting to get a better idea of what the painting was. Suddenly, her eyes went wide; she let out a squeal of excitement that made a lot of people in the crowd look back in her direction as she raised a hand to her mouth in shock. Then she ran to me, mouth wide open, with a shocked-but-happy expression on her face.

"Jim!" she exclaimed. "That's the freaking *Mona Lisa*!"

"*La Joconde* in French," I said, but I don't think she heard me. She was suddenly looking around the building with new eyes.

"Oh my…" she said, somewhat breathless. "This, this is the Louvre. We're in Paris! *Paris!!!*"

The hair on my arms began to rise as the air started becoming ionized. Electra, as her name implied, had power over electricity, and because of her excitement her control was starting to slip. I'd been on the receiving end of her electrical blasts before and had no desire to repeat the experience - even if it was an accident.

I raised my arm so she could see what was happening. It took her a second to realize what I was doing, and then her lips curved into a surprised "Oh!" Her brow furrowed in concentration for a second, and then the charge I'd felt building in the air suddenly dissipated. The danger past, Electra squealed again and jumped into my arms, giving me a bear hug.

****

With Paris being six hours ahead of us, we didn't have much time to see the museum. In fact, the Louvre normally would have been closed at the time we arrived, but I had checked and they had extended hours this particular weekend. Electra dragged me from one exhibit to the next, barely giving me time to view it before moving on. When they finally kicked the last of us visitors out at closing time - long before Electra and I had had a chance to see everything - it was dark outside, but she was still grinning from ear to ear.

"That was so awesome!" she screamed, spinning around in a circle with her arms outstretched.

"Yeah, we'll have to come back again and see the rest another time," I said.

"Come back?" she repeated, as if the thought hadn't occurred to her. Then she smiled and gave me an unexpected peck on the lips. *The shape of things to come, perhaps?*

"Next time, though, can we not teleport directly inside?" she asked. "I feel a little guilty about sneaking in without paying."

I laughed. "Admission's free for people under age eighteen. At worst, all we did was cut to the front of the line."

"Oh," she said, obviously rethinking the matter. "I guess that's not so bad. Regardless, no one's going to believe this when we get back."

"Well, we're not done yet," I said.

"We're not?"

"No. As they say, you haven't seen Paris until you've seen it at night."

We were still outside the Louvre, but I had slowly been guiding us in a particular direction as we walked. For the first time, Electra seemed to take a look around her. Although you could see the lights of the city in every direction, one object immediately caught her attention.

"Oh, Jim," she said matter-of-factly, "we can *not* leave without seeing *that*."

"Then you're in luck, because that's just where we're going. The Eiffel Tower."

****

The Tower was roughly two miles from the Louvre. I could have teleported us to it or picked Electra up and zoomed over there at Mach speed, but part of what makes certain events special is experiencing them to the fullest. Thus, we walked and talked until we reached our destination.

MUTATION

The Eiffel Tower is arranged in three levels. There's the top floor, which offers a remarkable view of Paris. Below that is the second floor, which contains, among other things, souvenir shops and the world-famous Jules Verne restaurant. Then there's the first floor, which also has shops and restaurants, as well as a variety of other activities.

We went to the top of the Tower first, taking the elevator (as opposed to having me teleport or fly us up). From there, we had a panoramic view of Paris. The city, lit up in a dazzling array of colors, was beautiful. Even so, I couldn't help but think that this girl with me, wind whipping gently through her hair, outshined even the City of Light. It was all I could do not to try to steal a kiss.

Next, we went down to the second floor to look for souvenirs. There's a widespread rumor that shopping with women is a horrid experience, but I rather enjoyed it – mostly because Electra spent most of the time goofing off. For instance, every time I turned away for a second, she'd slip away and spend the next few minutes hiding from me, dipping and dodging around souvenir displays and racks of clothes until I found her.

Once, when her attention was occupied by a miniature version of the Tower, I tried giving her a taste of her own medicine. Instead of hiding, however, I simply slapped a beret on my head and shifted, transforming my appearance to that of a stereotypical disdainful Frenchman in his mid-thirties. Then I walked up to Electra and took her hand in mine and kissed it smarmily. For a second she looked surprised, and then she burst out laughing and pulled her hand away.

MUTATION

"You can forget about holding my hand," she said between giggles, "until you change back. You look like a total lech!"

For a moment, I stood there stunned. How had she known it was me? I was so careful, making sure that she was looking away when I shifted, and as a shapeshifter the change was practically instantaneous.

"Oh," she said, pinching my cheek. "Is baby mad that Mommy saw through his little disguise? He must not remember who Mommy is."

As a reminder, she held up her hand and I saw a little bolt of electricity zip across her fingertips. Then it came back to me. Electra's power let her read bioelectric fields. In fact, those fields were as distinctive as photographs to her, and she could use them to distinguish people. Changing my appearance hadn't fooled her one bit. In fact, it had been Electra who - using that same power - had outed me as Kid Sensation a few weeks earlier, even when I was in another persona.

I shifted back and reached up to take the beret off.

"No, no, no," Electra protested. "Keep it on; it looks good on you." She pointed to a nearby beauty mirror sitting on a counter. "Take a look."

I walked over and glanced into the mirror. The reflection staring back at me showed a tall, slender sixteen-year-old guy with short, dark curly hair and a natural complexion that looked something in between fair and moderately tan. And she was right: the beret, oddly enough, did look good on me.

We left the shop shortly thereafter, with Electra buying the beret for me as a gift. (Or rather, I paid and she promised to pay me back.) On my part, I bought her an I-[Heart]-Paris t-shirt. We then went to dinner at *Le Jules Verne.*

The restaurant was rather upscale, so while *my* ensemble passed muster, the hostess went into a side closet and retrieved a ladies jacket for Electra. They kept such items on hand for occasions when patrons were not appropriately dressed, and I had to admit that it went a long way towards deemphasizing the casualness of Electra's attire. We were then seated at a window table, with a breathtaking view of the French capital.

The service was prompt and courteous (clearly an attempt to make up for the outrageous prices), and before long we had our appetizers – soup for me, salad for her – in front of us. However, it wasn't until we had our entrees that I decided to bring up something that had been nagging at me since we had left the safe house.

"So," I said nonchalantly, "do you recall when Vixen asked to speak to me this afternoon?"

She answered with a nod, barely taking her attention away from the shrimp pasta she had ordered.

"Did you notice," I continued, "that she called me your boyfriend?"

Again, Electra simply nodded, so I went on, a bit nervously. "Since you, uh, since you didn't correct her…does, uh, does that mean I'm your boyfriend?"

"Of course," she answered with a smile.

"So that means that you're my girlfriend?"

Her face suddenly took on an odd expression, twisted in a weird way by mock indignation. "Uh, have you *asked* me to be your girlfriend?"

"No."

"Then no, I'm not your girlfriend."

"But you just said that I'm your boyfriend."

"That's right."

I sat there, thoroughly confused. "So, you're saying I'm your boyfriend, but you're not my girlfriend."

"Yep."

I tossed my hands up in frustration. "How does that even work?"

She glanced upward for a moment, apparently deep in thought. "I'm not sure. It just does. I suppose you could say that you have obligations to me, but I don't have any to you. At least, not until you ask."

I let out an exasperated sigh. This is how women drive men crazy, this kind of incomprehensible feminine logic.

"Vy don ju keese har?" asked a voice next to me.

I turned and looked, paying attention for the first time to the people sitting at the table next to us. The way the dining room was set up, we had a table next to the window. Behind both me and Electra were other tables also lining the window. However, there was also a table next to us heading in towards the interior of the dining room.

Seated at the interior table was an elderly French couple, and they had the kind of visible affinity that only comes from long years together. The man, who was the person who had spoken, repeated his question, and this time I focused on what he was asking, filtering out his accent: "Why don't you kiss her?"

"Kiss her?" I asked.

"*Oui*," he said with a nod. "She is clearly in love, but wants you to express your love for her first. And why waste the moment? You make a reservation months in advance at a place as special as *Le Jules Verne*, and you will not tell her how you feel? It is foolishness!"

"Wait a minute," Electra said, "when did you make your reservations here?"

The couple looked at each other, and the man took the woman's hand in his before turning back to us. "It is our wedding anniversary. Fifty years. To make sure we celebrate in style, I make the reservation three months ago."

A frown suddenly darkened Electra's face. I was worried that the couple would take offense, so I picked up the thread of the conversation.

"Fifty years?" I asked, trying to appear both surprised and impressed. "How did you manage that?"

While I listened to the couple give me the secret of a long and happy relationship, I noticed Electra turn around and speak for a few seconds to the couple seated at the table behind her. Her face, if possible, looked even more distressed when she turned back to me.

"Please excuse me for a moment," she said, standing and placing her napkin on the table. Then she walked towards the hostess' stand – presumably to ask where the ladies' room was. Despite her departure, the old couple barely skipped a beat in telling me the story of their marriage.

They were still talking a few minutes later when I finally saw Electra reappear. However, instead of coming straight back to where we were seated, she seemed to wander the restaurant randomly, stopping to speak to other diners here and there. Finally, she came back to our table.

I took the opportunity to excuse myself. I had done my good deed for the day in listening to our fellow diners; Electra could take her turn in the salt mines now. (Okay, it wasn't *that* bad – and they actually had some useful words of wisdom – but I just didn't like the way she'd kind of deserted me.)

I went to the men's room, and when I came back the elderly couple had departed. Electra was picking idly at her food, still with a sullen look on her face. I sat down and reached out to her emphatically, and felt a roiling sea of conflicting emotions: anger, resentment, sadness, disappointment, and more. Something was seriously bothering her. I tried to get her to open up with some conversation, but she essentially shut me down at every turn with simple one-word responses to everything. ("Yes," "No," "Maybe," etc.)

"Okay," I finally said in frustration. "What is it?"

"What's what?"

"What is it that's got a stick up your butt? You've been in a foul mood ever since that old couple started speaking to us."

She looked like she was on the verge of denying it, and then something like resolve settled into her demeanor.

"Alright," she said. "Who is she?"

"Who's who?" I asked, baffled.

"The girl." When all she got from me was a confused look, she went on. "The *other* girl. The one you were originally going to bring here."

I shook my head, thoroughly nonplussed. "I don't know what you're talking about."

"At least have the decency not to lie about it!" she hissed. As she spoke, I noticed little sparks of electricity arcing through the tines of the fork she held.

"I'm not lying! I seriously have no idea what you're talking about, Electra!"

"You don't know what I'm talking about? Fine, we'll play it your way." She took a sip of water and continued. "That old couple said they had to book their reservation here a couple of months ago."

"Yeah, so what?"

"I also talked to the hostess. She said this is one of the most popular restaurants *in the world*, and the average reservation is made two months in advance."

"I'm still listening."

"I also asked some of the other diners – the ones I could find who spoke English – and they all made their reservations at least two months ago."

"Again, so what?"

"I didn't know you two months ago! And no, your shapeshifting into someone else that I may have met doesn't count. The bottom line is that you obviously intended to bring someone else here, and I don't appreciate being your back-up plan. Couldn't you at least have taken me somewhere else?"

I snorted derisively. "You've got this entire thing completely twisted. First of all, there's no other girl; there never was. You're the only one I've been interested in. Second, you're right; you do normally have to make reservations weeks in advance. However, I got a friend who's a cape to call in a favor. The restaurant is never at full capacity; they always leave room to accommodate bigwigs who drop in unannounced. Celebrities, heads of state, foreign dignitaries, superheroes.... They just have to pull out an extra table from the back. So I'm sorry that it wasn't necessary for me to jump through all kinds of hoops and make reservations months ahead of time just so you could feel important, princess!"

Over the course of my speech, Electra had slowly lowered her gaze until she was now staring at her plate and just playing with her food. It should have been enough, but I was still on my high horse. My grandfather was the one who had used his connections to get us a table here, so her baseless accusations were not just an attack on me, but an insult to him as well. I was about to continue when she looked up, eyes watery. I felt shame and sadness welling up in her.

"Jim, I'm sorry," she almost whispered. "It's just that...I like you, okay? And not the way I've liked guys in the past. There's something special about you, and I'm not talking about your powers. I just wanted you to think I was special, too, and thinking that you had planned this for some other girl made me feel that I wasn't."

Her apology kind of took the wind out of my sails in terms of anger. On an empathic level, it was heartfelt and sincere, something I couldn't overlook.

"I don't care what you felt or thought; you didn't have the right to accuse me of something like that," I said sternly.

"I know," she said, looking down again.

"It would serve you right if I just left and let you take a cab home."

She started to nod in agreement, but then frowned as the absurdity of my statement hit her. She looked up to find me grinning.

"You jerk," she said in clear relief, before playfully kicking me under the table. "You almost had me in tears."

"Well, I'm still mad at you. I'm just having a tough time showing it. And why should you care if I were bringing another girl here? It's not like you're my girlfriend."

That one earned me another connection between her foot and my shin, only this time there was a little less play and a little more kick. Following that, normal conversation between us resumed.

After dinner, I paid (leaving a generous tip on top of the already-expensive meal), and we left. Electra was keen to see more of the city, but I convinced her that we should get back. Although it was midnight by local time, it was only early evening back home. We had been gone about four hours thus far, and I was concerned that if we spent much more time in *Gay Paree* her circadian rhythm would get thrown off, giving her a teleportation version of jet lag.

My watch read 6:05 p.m. when I popped us back home, just outside the basement entrance to the safe house.

"Are you going to come up?" Electra asked.

It was still early, so it was a very tempting invitation – especially with her standing there facing me and looking incredibly beautiful. However, I really wanted to end things on a high note, so I declined.

"Anyway," she said, taking my hand, "this was fun. We should do it again."

"Yeah, but now you'll be expecting something grand every time we go out, so I've got to come up with something even better next time."

"Oh, are you worried that you set the bar too high? That nothing can top today? Well, let me put your mind at ease." She put a finger to her chin and glanced up as if she were giving the matter serious consideration. "It was okay, I guess."

"'Okay'? What is that, like two out of five stars? That's all I can get?"

"On the record, yeah. You can't expect a girl to show you all her cards just because you swooped her off to Paris. So that's the official verdict. It was an okay date."

I stepped a little closer to her. "And *un*officially?"

"Unofficially?" she repeated as if thinking about it. She put her hands around my neck and began leaning in closer to me. "Best. Date. Ever," she whispered, emphasizing each word in a way that made me struggle to keep my nervousness and excitement from being conspicuous.

She kissed me, long and lingering, making my head swim. Her lips were soft and inviting, like delicate rose petals being gently crushed as I pulled her closer. She tasted delicious – some provocative combination of sugar and honey that sent a jolt through my nerve endings, setting them on fire.

It wasn't until we separated a few moments later that I realized that it hadn't all been in my mind; the air was charged, crackling with electricity. It took a few seconds for Electra to notice, but as soon as she did, the air became de-ionized.

"Sorry," she said demurely, lowering her eyes as she pushed back a stray strand of hair. You didn't have to be an empath to see that she was slightly embarrassed at losing control.

"You know," I said, taking her hand. "Maybe I will come in for a bit."

She smiled.

MUTATION

Chapter 7

Our date ended with me and Electra going up to the safe house common area and watching TV for a few hours. I had thought that ending the date right after returning from Paris was the high-water mark, but it turns out that snuggling on a couch was a lot better. We said our goodbyes - punctuated by another kiss - after agreeing to call each other the next day. I went home on cloud nine and slept like a baby.

The next morning saw me finally get around to packing for my upcoming stay at the Academy. I wasn't leaving for a few more days, but Mom would start to fret if I waited until the last minute. Packing, in and of itself, wasn't particularly difficult. The hard part was figuring out what to take.

Living in-residence, we would be wearing Academy-issued uniforms most of the time. Outside of class, we'd also have Academy-themed sweats, t-shirts, etc. Long story short, there wasn't a need to bring a lot of your own clothes; in fact, the Academy's recommendation was that students only bring about seven different outfits, plus a set of formal wear.

Bearing all that in mind, I thought that I'd done an excellent job with respect to the clothes I'd planned to take with me. However, the day before I was to leave, Mom decided to make a surprise inspection of my bag.

"Oh, no!" she screeched in horror, pulling out a threadbare pair of jeans. "These pants practically have a hole in the knee!"

"But that's the style now, Mom," I whined.

"Since when do you care about style and what's in fashion?" she asked. I simply shrugged, and she went on plowing through my clothes. "And what's going on with this ratty t-shirt?"

"It's one of my favorites!"

"Not anymore," she said, and tossed it into the wastebasket I kept in my room.

One by one, she went through each article of clothing and found something distasteful about almost every one of them.

"Jim," she said when finished, having stacked all of the clothes she didn't like into one big pile, "this entire wardrobe is shameful. You are *not* going to go off to the Academy and embarrass this family by wearing any of this trash." She waved a hand at the mound of clothes.

I was on the verge of protesting when I detected a surging tide of emotion within her: love, warmth, affection, pride, fear. Having felt it before, I recognized it for what it was - her maternal instincts coming to the fore. The issue with the clothes was less about how appropriate they were and more about her need to still be "Mom" to me, to know that she was still needed. With that in mind, I ultimately let her shove a credit card into my hand as she told me to go to the mall and get some "nice, new things."

****

It was a little after one o'clock in the afternoon when I finally got to the mall. I was fairly excited about being there - not because I love shopping, but rather because this little excursion had an extra bit of excitement: I got to drive myself there.

Originally, I had planned to get there via teleportation, which is the most convenient form of travel for me. However, my grandfather had offered me the use of his car. Of course, he knew I wasn't licensed, but he pooh-poohed the notion of that being a barrier to me driving.

"Listen to me," he'd said. "Everybody driving around out there at some point in time got behind the wheel - unsupervised - before they were licensed. It's just one of those things that everyone experiences."

With that, he'd given me the keys, but not without one final admonition. "Still, if the cops pull you over, I'm a doddering old man and you took my car without permission."

Thus I found myself in my grandfather's sedan, parking on one of the upper levels of the mall's multi-level garage. Even though traveling in a car was the equivalent of a snail's pace compared to my usual mode of transport, I'd be lying if I said there wasn't a certain thrill attached to driving around without a license - the same rush people often get when they're doing something that they're not supposed to.

The shopping itself took almost no time at all. One of the benefits of being a shapeshifter is that you never have to find clothes that fit you perfectly; if you like it, you can just buy it - no need to waste time trying it on - and always shift your body to conform, if necessary. That said, I prefer to get clothes that are close to my natural state. Still, I was finished in roughly an hour, having found some jeans, shirts, and tennis shoes that I felt would make my mother happy (and convince her that I wasn't living like a vagabond while at the Academy).

I was walking back to the sedan, shopping bags in hand, when my cell phone rang. Ordinarily, that would have been uncommon; being a teleporter, it's just as easy for me to have a face-to-face with someone as it is to call them - easier, in fact. However, since I'd started dating Electra, my cell had been getting more of a workout. (Apparently, while girls might be willing to talk to you when they first wake up in the morning, they don't necessarily want you seeing them that early, or at other inopportune times.)

As we actually had a date for that night - our last before heading to the Academy - I naturally expected the call to be from Electra. It wasn't. Instead, when I pulled out my phone and looked at the screen, it read "Caller ID Blocked."

I frowned. My phone actually came equipped with a feature called Anonymous Caller Rejection. Basically, if a caller tried to mask or block their own number, my phone wouldn't put their call through. That being the case, my curiosity was piqued. I hit the "Talk" button.

"Hello?" I asked.

"Kid Sensation," said a voice I immediately recognized. "This is Mr. Gray."

I grunted annoyingly in response. I was getting close to my grandfather's car. I had my bags in one hand and was holding the phone to my ear with the other, so I telekinetically pulled the keys from my pocket and hit the button to unlock the doors.

"You shouldn't have to announce yourself," I said flatly, "because you aren't supposed to be able to call this phone anonymously."

He laughed. "That's a minor inconvenience that's no trouble for us to get around."

"And the dozen or so FCC laws that you're breaking in the process, I suppose they're just minor inconveniences, too." I telekinetically pushed the button on the keyring to pop the sedan's trunk open.

Gray sighed, ignoring my comment. "I had really hoped this call wouldn't be necessary."

"What do you mean?" I asked as I tossed my bags into the trunk and slammed it shut.

"You were supposed to call me before you left for the Academy. I've yet to hear from you."

"Well, I don't leave until tomorrow." I walked to the driver's door. "And I've still got your card in my wallet" - which was true - "so I think you'd agree that I still had time."

"True. Yet somehow I feel that you've already made a decision about my request."

I debated for a second. I had no intention of being his flunky, so why pussyfoot around about it?

"That would be a correct assumption. I don't think we could form a compatible working relationship."

"I see," he said, almost disappointedly. "And there's nothing I can say that can change your mind?"

"That's a big ten-four, good buddy," I flippantly acknowledged as I opened the driver-side door.

There was silence on his end for a moment, and then a calm, "If that's the way you want it."

The line went dead, but there was something about his tone when he'd last spoke...oh well, I wasn't going to waste time worrying about it.

I tossed my cell phone into the empty cupholder between the two front seats, where it rattled around for a second. Then I put my foot into the car and started to bend down, preparing to get in. A sudden movement out of the corner of my eye caught my attention, but before I could turn my head and fully register what it was,

MUTATION

something smashed into my chest like a jackhammer, knocking the wind out of me and sending me airborne.

MUTATION

Chapter 8

Backwards, I flew across the garage like a shot from a gun. I caromed off the windshield of a nearby car, smashing it as I ricocheted away like a wildly fired bullet. Somewhat dazed and totally confused, I was still trying to get my bearings when my momentum was suddenly arrested by something like a rocket blasting into my midsection. What little air remaining in my lungs came out in an agonizing gasp as my body wrapped limply around whatever had slammed into my stomach.

I still couldn't think straight, didn't know exactly what was happening, but one thing was certain: I was under attack. Instinct and training took over.

I went into super speed, a blatant attempt to buy time while I tried to assess exactly what was going on. The world around me quickly decelerated, going into extreme slow motion like someone hitting the pause button on a DVR. I took a deep breath and nearly screamed in anguish. The pain in my chest and stomach were excruciating; sucking in air was like breathing fire. I ignored the pain and looked around.

Off to one side, I saw a young couple, apparently headed towards their car. The man was staring at me in shock, and had dropped the shopping bags he had been carrying. From my perspective, the bags hung there, frozen in mid-air between the hand that had let them go and the ground. The woman, whose mouth had fallen open, appeared to be in the process of raising a hand to her lips to stifle a gasp.

Not far away, I saw a woman in the process of putting a toddler into a carseat. Although the woman, with her back to me, was oblivious to what was going on, the toddler was looking over her shoulder and pointing in my direction. That suddenly reminded me to take stock of my own position.

I was still up in the air, but not flying. Instead, I was being held there in the large, meaty paw of a giant. The man was at least seven feet tall, and was dressed in a black muscle shirt and some kind of dark pants that seemed military grade. He was clean-shaven and bald, making his age somewhat ambiguous, but from the wrinkles in his brow and creases in his face, I pegged him as early forties. He was wearing a weird set of goggles over his eyes and an earpiece.

He was incredibly massive, with a broad, impressive bulk to match his height. His neck was like a tire rim, and his biceps like tree trunks. In short, over-sized and over-muscled, everything about him screamed super-strong brawler. (Not to mention the fact that his grip on my midsection was like a set of steel pincers.)

From the angle and set of his body – as well as the manner in which he held me – I could tell he was preparing to smash me into the ground. However, something didn't make sense.

The giant holding me was, like everyone else in the garage, moving so slowly that he might as well have been a mannequin. The blow that had first hit me had essentially come out of nowhere, but with such speed that I didn't even have time to counter it. That meant…

I looked around wildly. *There!* Motion over in the direction that I had come from – by my grandfather's car. With everything else practically frozen in time, it was easy to pick out.

It was a young guy, maybe in his twenties, with dark wavy hair. He had on the same kind of goggles and earpiece as his brawny companion, but also wore some type of body armor. From my perspective, he appeared to be jogging leisurely in our direction, but in real time he had to be moving at super speed.

So, this was presumably the guy who had initially hit me. He must have been moving incredibly fast for me not to have seen him coming. Angrily, I mentally marked a tally for him, but since I didn't know his name, I dubbed him "Swifty." Likewise for his muscular companion, whom I designated "Brawny."

I reached for them both with my teleportation power, ready to put them on the dark side of the moon. (Okay, maybe not the dark side of the moon, but some place remote, like Antarctica - a trip that would evoke the mantra of "know your enemy" the next time they thought about attacking someone without provocation.) I was just about to send them on their way when a few ugly memories reared up.

I had teleported people in anger before - unintentionally, on a couple of occasions. Thus, there existed the very real possibility that I could indeed transport Swifty and Brawny somewhere completely inhospitable if I let my emotions run away with me. If I couldn't control myself, even with bad apples like these, I was dangerous to everyone around me - including innocent civilians. I needed to take a second.

I switched back to normal speed, then phased just before Brawny smacked me into the concrete floor. I went with the momentum of his motion, going straight through the floor to the level immediately below the one on which I had parked. There was a dull but audible smack as Brawny's hand must have connected with the garage floor above me, causing dust to billow out and scaring a group of pigeons into flight from the rafters. People heading for their cars ducked and ran for cover, fearing the place was collapsing.

I had stopped myself before coming into contact with the ground on this level; now I rested there, floating in mid-air, taking a moment to make sure I had a firm grip on my temper before I engaged these guys again. When I was certain that I wouldn't do anything irreversible with my teleportation power, I got ready to zoom back up through the roof to the floor above. Before I did that, however, I noticed someone else coming down - actually phasing through the floor as I had.

In actuality, there were four of them. There were Swifty and Brawny, but also another man and a woman. The other man wore the same type of body armor as Swifty. Tall and slender, he had brown hair that was starting to go gray at the temples. He had dark beady eyes and a beak-like nose that, all in all, gave him the semblance of a buzzard.

The woman was a different story entirely. She had short blond hair cut into bangs that framed a face of soft, delicate features. She wore a skin-tight, white bodice that accentuated all of her feminine attributes. Finally, she was literally radiant - she was covered in a soft, fine glow that pulsed around her like an echoing heartbeat.

Like Swifty and Brawny, these latest arrivals also wore earpieces and the same odd goggles, which I now recognized as having IR lenses. The four dropped down, in insubstantial form, until their feet touched the ground, and then they solidified and fanned out.

A few mall shoppers stood around, watching the spectacle as events unfolded. Several of the smarter ones, however, recognizing that a battle between supers was brewing and about to bubble over, took off for the interior of the mall, trying to put as much distance as possible between themselves and the prospect of wholesale carnage.

Although they were facing my direction, the four didn't seem to be fully focused on me. Quickly, I opened myself up empathically, reaching out to each of them simultaneously to see what I could sense. Oddly enough, although they had varying feelings underneath, I detected almost the same emotional state coming from the surface of their individual psyches: a high level of attentiveness - a sense of being completely alert, as if they were listening to something.

Still angry but feeling more in control, I reached for them, preparing to make them all next-door-neighbors with Emperor penguins, and found my power closing on...nothing. They had vanished.

Or rather, three of them had - the men. The woman just stood there, smiling at me with a sly expression that made my hair stand on end - as if she knew something I didn't. Willing to take what I could get, I focused on her, tried to teleport her. Again nothing happened; this time, however, I understood what had occurred, as well as what the woman's secret was: she was a teleporter.

The entire gist of being a teleporter is that you can go or be anywhere you want. By extension, you *don't* have to go any place where you *don't* want to be. By way of example, if you could somehow transport a teleporter from Point A to Point B, their own teleportation power would immediately bring them back to Point A if that's where they wanted to be. In short, you can't teleport a teleporter against their will, and there's a null effect when one teleporter tries to do so to another.

All of this flashed through my brain in an instant. Knowing her secret was out, the woman winked at me, then raised a hand in my direction. Almost immediately, a focal point of light gathered at her fingertips, and then shot in my direction with laser-like intensity.

I phased, and the laser beam passed harmlessly through me, striking and scorching one of the concrete beams near the ceiling instead. However, the use of her laser triggered something in my brain, and suddenly, I knew who this woman was.

Her name was Estrella; she was a well-known merc - a super who hired out to the highest bidder. Coming so close on the heels of my conversation with Gray, she had to be working for him, along with the rest of her compatriots. Her power set revolved around light and heat, and included the ability to fly. She was not someone to take lightly - especially when you considered that she could also teleport.

Bearing that in mind, I shifted into super speed and flew at her, arm cocked back to deliver a punishing blow. Not being a speedster herself, Estrella wouldn't be able to avoid me; I'd be on her before she could even teleport. At the last second, however, some chivalrous impulse took hold of me, making me abhor the idea of hitting a woman. Thus, I changed tactics and instead tried to tackle her around the middle. My arms, however, closed on nothing.

The miss threw me off-balance, and I banged against the side of a parked car before reversing my momentum.

What the…?

I didn't know what had happened. I couldn't have missed her, and she hadn't teleported. In fact, she was turning to face me now, with that evil, I-know-something-you-don't-know grin on her face.

Of course! She had phased!

I'd completely forgotten that they had phased down from the upper floor of the garage just a few moments a–

A brutal shoulder hit from Swifty cut off my thought processes and sent me crashing into a concrete column nearby, where I smacked my head hard enough to get an immediate headache. Suddenly, I heard a grunt and felt wild emotions surging near me, an almost palpable bloodlust. Disoriented but recognizing the danger, I teleported wildly, popping myself about twenty feet away just as Brawny made a flying tackle at the spot where I'd just been.

He hit the garage column like a wrecking ball, the force of his impact sending tremors throughout the structure. The column shattered, sending broken chunks of concrete skittering across the garage floor like pieces of eggshell as car alarms started going off like klaxons.

Somehow, I had foolishly forgotten about Estrella's companions. She had initially teleported them away from me, but I guess I'd gotten it into my head that she wasn't going to bring them back - an idiotic assumption on my part.

The column Brawny had destroyed was obviously a load-bearing structure (or maybe he'd done more damage than I initially realized), because an ominous creak sounded, followed by a thunderous crack. Part of the ceiling slab gave way, bending down at an angle that let two cars from above roll down with crushing force onto a sports car and an SUV. Ceiling lights began to flicker all across this level of the garage; a pipe near the broken ceiling slab burst without warning, spewing water out in a wide arc.

This turn of events had an unsettling effect on the crowd of spectators. From the moment Brawny took out the column, they'd all suddenly realized that they had pressing business elsewhere and scattered towards the exits, screaming.

It only took a few moments to take all this in, but the headache I'd picked up was making it hard to focus. I teleported outside - up to the roof of the garage - as much to get away from Estrella and her crew as to clear my head. But if that was my wish, it was in vain, because she immediately popped up next to me.

This time, I swung without hesitation, all thoughts of chivalry banished. Again, I failed to connect because she was phased, and I stumbled, off-balance. She took the opportunity to wallop me with a backhand that lifted me off my feet. I didn't travel far, though, as Brawny caught me, wrapping his arms around me in a crushing bear hug that made it feel like my ribs were dry twigs on the verge of snapping. Screaming in pain, I teleported back into the garage, not too far from where the broken pipe was still gushing water. As if on cue, Estrella and company teleported back inside as well. I went invisible - something I should have done much earlier - then phased through a classic sixties Mustang convertible and lay down in the back seat, trying to get a moment to think.

I was getting creamed. They had clearly brought their A-game, and had had me on the ropes from the start. Moreover, I hadn't been able to lay a finger on any of them. I'd been trained in how to fight multiple adversaries at once, but I'd never encountered anything like this before. They were outmaneuvering me at every turn. It was as if they were psychic...

As soon as the thought occurred to me, I knew that to be precisely what it was. The way Estrella knew exactly when to teleport her team, their ability to follow me when *I* teleported, the precise timing of their phasing...they had a precognitive on their side. (It also explained their peculiar emotional state, why it seemed like they were listening to someone. Apparently they were.)

Precogs and clairvoyants often make for extremely difficult opponents. There are few greater advantages than knowing exactly what your adversary will do. Still, my grandfather had taught me a few tricks for getting the better of them. However, it helped to know something about the precise nature of their powers.

Precognitive abilities could vary wildly. Some could see a specific future; others could only see probabilities. One might have control of their power to see what will happen; another might not and simply live with visions coming to them at random times. Regardless, precogs typically came in one of two flavors: their ability to see the future was usually either long-and-narrow, or short-and-broad.

With respect to the former, precogs in that category could see far into the future, but only with respect to limited subjects - e.g., they could see what the future held regarding a particular person, event, and so on, but not for anyone or anything else. For example, a precog might be able to tell you if your favorite sports team will make it to the championship game that's scheduled six months from now, but they can't tell you how any other sports franchise will fare. Basically, they had tunnel vision to a certain extent

In the short-and-broad category, precogs could see what would occur with respect to just about any person, event, location, etc., but only within a very limited time frame. They might be able to see ten minutes into the future, or maybe just ten seconds.

Outside the Mustang, Estrella and her team stalked through the garage in silence. Having switched my vision over to infrared, I saw them as crimson and scarlet forms, methodically hunting for prey they knew to be hiding somewhere nearby. They were obviously looking for me, but it seemed that their precog was having trouble pinning me down at the moment. *Score one for invisibility!*

Having bought myself a little time, the obvious question now was, what were the particular facets of this precog's ability? I needed to find out, and that meant finding the precog in question. They could be anywhere, but odds were they were close; proximity to the action seemed to increase a precog's odds of accurately predicting what would occur. I reached out with my empathic ability, casting a wide net, uncertain of what I was looking for.

I ignored the adrenaline-laced sensations from Estrella and her cohorts. Likewise with the mall patrons, many of whom were feeling fright and panic - and in some cases hysteria. I went further, still looking for…I'm not sure what, just something out of the ordinary.

I'd never tried to read this far out before, and I was getting ready to withdraw when I felt it. It was an odd sensation - something akin to fervent excitement, but more like the emotional equivalent of a hyperactive child trying to get a parent's attention: "Look at me! Look at me! Look at me! Look at me!"

It originated from the other side of the mall - a surface parking lot near the back that saw limited use since the parking garage had been built. Telepathically, I peeked inside the mind of the person who was sending the emotional broadcast.

<Finally! Took you long enough!> said a mental voice that I pegged as belonging to a child - a girl.

<What???> I was a little confused. I had tried to tiptoe into her mind, but had obviously been heard.

<I mean, I thought you'd *never* figure it out - and I can see the future!>

<Wait a minute! You're the psychic? The precognitive? What are you, like seven?>

<I'm ten!> she stated indignantly. <And you'd better be nice if you want my help!>

<And why would you do that?>

<Because I need *you* to help *me*. I'm Rudi, by the way.> At that moment, I got an image of her as well - a young girl with an olive complexion, green eyes, and curly brown hair.

This was interesting; I hadn't expected the precog to be on my side. <I'm listening, but you need to make this quick. I'm kind of in the middle of something.>

<We have a few minutes. See?>

I felt a kind of mental nudging and peeked out of the Mustang's window. A group of about a half-dozen mall cops had shown up and had their weapons drawn on Estrella's team. The security guards were clearly outmatched, but kudos to them for trying to do their job. It also occurred to me that, with my pursuers preoccupied, this would be a good time to put some distance between me and them, and I shared that with Rudi.

<Forget about it,> she said. <It won't work.>

<Why not?>

<Because I'm the clairvoyant and I said it won't! Look, we don't have a lot of time, so we can either waste it having me explain why that plan won't work, or we can discuss some things that will help you form one that will.>

I certainly had to acknowledge that teleporting hadn't been a big help to me thus far. That being the case, I hesitated only a moment before acquiescing.

<Well, you're right about one thing - the Keystone Cops over there won't buy us much time,> I noted, indicating the security guards. <So, if you've got a plan, you'd better talk fast.>

<Okay, there's a team of four of them. The leader's a woman called–>

<Estrella.> I cut her off. <I got that. What about the speedster, Swifty?>

I heard her laugh, mentally, at the nickname I'd given him. At the same time, I heard a hollow sound - like a weird echo - in the background of her thoughts. <He's called Blitz. The strong one is Brick. The last one is Spectre.>

<Spectre? I take it he's the one with the phasing ability?>

<That's a big ten-four, good buddy.> She giggled.

I frowned, not liking what I'd learned at all. Collectively, Estrella's team mimicked a bunch of my own powers, meaning they were probably assembled specifically to deal with me. Moreover, they had a precog on their side, Rudi, who – based on her last response –

had obviously foreseen my conversation with Gray. That brought up the subject of her abilities.

<Your powers,> I said. <How far out can you see?>

<It varies. It depends on different things, such as how tired I am. Like right now, since I've been at it for a while today, it's about five or six seconds.>

<But you can consciously control it?>

<Usually, but sometimes a vision will just hit me out of the blue.>

Not far away, an obviously nervous mall cop — probably the head of security — was engaged in a heated war of words with Estrella. I continued my conversation with Rudi while keeping an eye on them. <When you use your power, what do you see?>

She was silent for a few seconds. <I see scenes…sometimes regarding a person, sometimes a location. They play out like a movie in my head.>

<So, you can see me now? While I'm invisible?>

<No, although I can get a sense of where you are — like I know you're still in the garage right now.> There was the weird echo in her head again, and then she resumed talking. <As I said, it's like a movie. I can't see you, but if you were to do something - like pick up a stick - I'd see that.>

Interesting. While I thought about it, the odd echo in her mind sounded again. This time, I listened closely - and almost jumped out my skin.

<That voice in the background!> I shouted. <It's you! It's you *talking*! You're still helping them find me?>

<Yeah.> There was a matter-of-fact tone to her voice, as if she'd be doing anything else.

<How can you do that???!!!>

\<It's called multi-tasking. Duh.\> Mentally she rolled her eyes.

\<No, I mean how can you be helping *them* when you claim you want to help *me*?\>

\<I have to! They have Josh!\>

\<Who?\>

\<Josh. My little brother. They're holding him to make me do what they say. That's what I need your help with. I help you, and you help us get away.\>

\<Deal,\> I said, with barely any hesitation. \<But why can't you just lie? Tell them I'm up on the roof or something?\>

\<Oh, that's brilliant. And what do you think happens when I tell them something like you just teleported to the roof, and when they follow you're not there?\>

\<Okay, you've made your point.\> As I watched, Estrella and her team had apparently grown weary of talking. They went into motion, fully engaging the security guards. \<We're almost out of time; what's your plan?\>

\<Plan? What plan? I don't have any plan.\>

Understandably, I was confused. \<Then what was all that talk about helping me???!!!\>

\<I just gave you a bunch of information about Estella's team and my powers. You're the great Kid Sensation! Figure something out!\>

The mall security guards went down. I needed to come up with something fast. The echo sounded in Rudi's mind. To be so young, she was obviously immensely talented to not only be able to see the future, but to also carry on a mental conversation that was different that the verbal one she was having. An idea sprang into my head.

<You're running out of time!> Rudi sounded desperate. <They're engaging thermal sensors!>

Of course - the IR goggles they were wearing. They knew I was still there but couldn't see me, so they were going to try to locate me by body heat. I almost laughed out loud (obviously they didn't know *everything* about me), then lowered my core body temperature before turning back to the thought I'd just had.

<You're not telepathic,> I stated. <That means you have to tell them everything verbally. That's why they have the earpieces.>

<Yes.>

<But you can only talk so fast, right? You can only say so much at one time?>

<I guess...>

That was all I needed to know. I waited a few seconds, then became visible, teleported, and started counting.

One thousand one...

I popped into existence near the busted water pipe – just far enough away to avoid getting wet. Telekinetically, I ripped about a three-foot section of it loose and grabbed it. The weight felt good in my hand.

One thousand two...

Rudi could only see about seven seconds into the future. Since I was visible now, she could undoubtedly see me and was telling Estrella's team (whom I could see spread out across this level of the garage) where to find me. My goal now was to overload her with information – move so fast that she couldn't convey it quickly enough.

One thousand three...

MUTATION

I teleported, popping up behind Estrella. I swung with the pipe at the back of her head.

One thousand four...

The pipe passed harmlessly through her; she'd been phased. I teleported–

One thousand five...

–and popped up by Blitz. I shifted into super speed, swinging the pipe so fast that it made a humming noise in the air. But Blitz was already zipping away, and was safely out of harm's way by the time the pipe passed through where he had been.

One thousand six...

I teleported directly in front of Brick. I swung hard, but only made a slight connection before my target disappeared – apparently teleported by Estrella. With so little of the force of my swing transferring into the blow, he probably didn't even feel it.

One thousand seven...

I teleported behind Spectre. This was the moment of truth. If I was right, then all my hopscotching around – teleporting from one of these guys to the next in quick succession and going on the offensive each time – should have been more than Rudi was able to get out in a verbally coherent fashion. (I imagined her rattling off information in staccato bursts, like a machine gun unloading, as she tried to get everything out: he's-going-to-teleport-over-by-the-broken-pipe-and-now-he's-going-by-Estrella...next-look-for-him-to-pop-up-next-to-Blitz-and-right-after-that-then-he's-going-to...)

I swung the pipe...and was rewarded with a sound like a firecracker as it connected with the back of Spectre's skull. He dropped like a sack of potatoes.

Unexpectedly, there was a scream of anguish from nearby. It was Estrella. The way the sound came out of her, you'd have thought it was her that I'd hit.

She raised a hand and fired a laser beam at me. I shifted into super speed and stepped aside as it went past and struck a directional sign on a nearby wall. The sign must have had some kind of reflective coating, because the beam dispersed, radiating out in the form of a score of smaller lights that formed a brilliant kaleidoscope.

Estrella teleported next to Spectre. She screamed again, this time more in fury than anything else. Standing over him, she raised both hands and fired, like a gunfighter in the Old West trying to unload on an enemy. Running at super speed, I was easily able to avoid her blasts. Other parts of the garage weren't so lucky, as lasers carved chunks out of nearby walls, sliced through columns, and even struck the gas tank of a station wagon, causing it to blow up.

Not far away, I saw Blitz also zig and zag to avoid Estrella's blasts. I almost laughed as I realized what was happening. At our speed, we were both nothing but blurs to her, so she was firing indiscriminately. I then pulled one of my favorite stunts with speedsters – I telekinetically tripped him.

Blitz went down flailing, bouncing along the ground until he slammed into a car. Suddenly, I felt an emotional void – a vacuum where just a moment before there had been a fiery storm. I looked around; Estrella had disappeared, as had Spectre.

Something I did notice, however, were the downed security guards. With me actually able to get into the mix now, this was the last place anyone needed to be lying around unconscious. I teleported them all into one of the stores where I'd gone shopping just a short time earlier. There was bound to be some panic at a bunch of coldcocked mall cops popping up out of nowhere, and for a second I wondered why Estrella hadn't just teleported them somewhere out of the way rather than have her team take them on.

I didn't have time to dwell on it, however, as my peripheral vision picked up movement. Turning in that direction, I saw Brick bearing down on me. I went invisible, and when he slowed to check his charge, I walloped him with the pipe, which I had also made invisible and was still holding. He swung in my direction, but I avoided him easily, then hit him again.

And so we danced for a few seconds – him swinging and missing, me following up with a lick from the pipe. I doubt that it hurt him very much – it was probably on par with a bee sting – but it still had to be maddening, as evidenced by the fact that he just started swinging wildly in all directions.

I took a step back from Brick's wild gyrations and looked around for Blitz. He was back on his feet again, but when he tried to run, I tripped him again before he got five steps. He went tumbling along the ground again. I did the same thing when he got up and tried to run the next time.

It went on that way for a few moments, with me alternating between hitting Brick with the pipe and telekinetically tripping Blitz every time he moved. I occasionally glanced around to make sure Estrella hadn't come back, but she didn't put in another appearance. Without her and Spectre, a significant portion of their arsenal seemed to be gone.

For a second, however, I wondered if Rudi could still predict my movements. That's when I looked and noticed that Blitz no longer had his earpiece; it had apparently been lost during one of the occasions when I tripped him. Brick still had his, but was so obviously enraged that he probably wasn't listening even if Rudi was trying to tell him something. He was now picking up cars and tossing them around randomly, grunting with the effort. The low garage ceiling made it difficult for him to get a lot of distance with his throws, but he still got an *A* for effort as the cars he threw smashed into and demolished other vehicles (as well as parts of the building itself).

It was a good thing we were in a relatively inexpensive parking garage. It would be a shame if this kind of damage were taking place in an expensive structure like an office building or a museum...

I was hit with a sudden inspiration. Without taking time to fully think it through, I teleported myself, Brick, and Blitz.

We popped up in a huge room, much like the one I had teleported myself and Electra to for our date. In fact, this was indeed the Louvre again, although a different section. It was an area that Electra and I had peeked into but been unable to enter as it was undergoing renovations.

Looking around now, I could see that the area was still closed to the public. Natural light cascaded down through a ceiling made up almost entirely of panes of glass. There was no artwork in the room, although there were a number of pedestals (presumably for statues) and wooden benches bolted to the floor. Moreover, a group of men in coveralls were hard at work painting one of the far walls when we showed up, although none of them seemed to notice us initially.

If he was aware of the change in environment – going from a dark garage to a well-lit room – Brick didn't show it particularly well. However, just to keep him in the right frame of mind, I – while still invisible – went over and smacked him good and hard on the knee with the pipe.

Brick howled, then reached over and gripped a huge stone pedestal that was at least four feet wide and three feet high. With a massive effort, he wrenched it up from the floor and then threw it in the direction where he apparently believed I was standing. It flew through the air fifty feet, then crashed down and went skidding across the floor, plowing up exorbitantly expensive tile along the way.

The workmen took one look and ran helter skelter for the nearest exit, shouting anxiously in French. A few seconds later an alarm began blaring, and metal bars descended over the room's exits. The place was going into lockdown.

Brick ripped another pedestal up and flung it as well, then pulled up a bench that he began swinging like a baseball bat. His swings were ferocious but uncoordinated, like a batter trying to nail a bunch of wild pitches. Obviously, he was after me, hoping to get a lucky hit in.

Maybe Brick hadn't noticed the change of scenery or the alarms, but Blitz obviously had. He ran to his teammate, trying to calm him. Brick, however, was seemingly in no mood to talk. He swung the bench at Blitz, who tried to zip out of the way. Unfortunately for Blitz, I took that moment to telekinetically lift him about a foot into the air. Unable to touch the ground with his feet, Blitz couldn't get any traction. In short, he couldn't move.

The bench connected with Blitz right around the hip. Limply, he flew across the room like a cannonball before cratering into a wall. Comically, he stuck there for a second, embedded, before sliding bonelessly to the floor.

Brick seemed stunned for a second, surprised that he had actually made contact. His eyes darted around the room, and for the first time he seemed to become aware of the fact that he was in an entirely different place - and that an alarm was going off. He didn't have long to ponder, however, as a sound like a Harrier jet thundered outside the building, drowning out the alarms and causing the glass panes in the ceiling to rattle violently. Two of those panes shattered and came raining down as a streak of crimson burst through the ceiling.

The French were notoriously protective of their *objets d'art* - especially those on display in the Louvre. Rumor was that a French super was always on standby to lend a hand should anyone attempt to steal anything from the world-famous museum. Whether true or not, there was no denying that someone had responded in near-record time to the commotion being made by Brick.

It was Rouge, a world-renowned French superhero. He was a slender man, without a lot of obvious muscle or weight. Moreover, he was a little on the short side - probably five-nine or so. He had slick, dark hair that he wore combed back, revealing a rather prominent forehead. All in all, if one were to go by appearances, he wasn't particularly impressive.

MUTATION

As they say, however, appearances can be deceiving, and that was rarely more true than with Rouge. Despite his uninspiring physique, he was generally counted among the top ten supers on the planet. Moreover, his name, Rouge, was not just a nod to the bright red outfit he always wore, but also alluded to the fact that he had an infamously short temper. More than a few supervillains, upon seeing him in person, had thought his reputation exaggerated, only to find out that - if anything - it was grossly understated.

It now looked like Brick's name was going to be added to that list. Anticipating a possible brawl, I cycled through various portions of the light spectrum until my vision found something approaching normal.

Rouge said something to Brick in French, which the latter obviously didn't understand. Rouge seemed to repeat himself, only this time his words were accompanied by hand gestures, as he seemed to indicate that Brick should put down the bench, which he was still holding.

The scene was almost comical. The disparity in their appearances - height, weight, bulk, etc. - made it seem as if the hulkish Brick was being admonished by a child. It was all I could do not to laugh out loud.

Despite the fact that he didn't seem to speak French, Brick apparently had no problem interpreting Rouge's tone. He snarled in response, then swung the bench like he was trying to bat one out of the park. There was an explosive crack as the wooden bench didn't just break, but actually splintered upon coming into contact with Rouge. Slivers of wood went flying in all directions. Brick stood holding the remnants of the bench in his hands, as if unsure of what had just happened.

On his part, Rouge had never moved. Brick might as well have hit him with a feather for all the effect it seemed to have. Rouge calmly looked himself over, brushed a few splinters from the shoulder of his costume - then exploded into action.

He slammed a fist into Brick's belly that made the larger man double over in obvious pain. Then Rouge brought his knee up, nailing Brick on the chin and causing him to flip over onto his back. He followed this up by reaching down and grabbing Brick around one of his ankles, then picked him up and repeatedly slammed him to the ground in a back-and-forth fashion, as if Brick were a rug he was trying to beat the dust out of.

Rouge's onslaught didn't stop there, but I had seen enough. On a personal note, I decided that Rouge's reputation regarding his temper was well-deserved. Moreover, as I wasn't fully aware of his power set, I decided to make my exit - just in case he could somehow sense my presence.

I turned my attention to Blitz before I left, but he was still out cold. I smiled to myself, thinking how upset Gray would be that his team had failed to take me. At the thought, an impertinent impulse came over me. I took the card Gray had given me, made it visible, and surreptitiously tucked it into one of Blitz's pockets. Then I teleported back to the mall.

MUTATION

Chapter 9

My first thought was to follow up on my promise to get Rudi and her brother. I had popped up, invisible, at the back parking lot. I reached out telepathically; this time, finding her was a piece of cake since I knew what I was looking for.

<Alright,> I said. <Two of your playmates are down for their naps.>

<Yay!!!> She mentally clapped her hands with glee. <For a second there, I wasn't sure you'd be able to do it. After all, combined, they seemed a pretty good match for you.>

<That's on paper. But in reality you have to remember that the whole is greater than the sum of its parts.>

I could feel her pondering that, but it was something she could figure out later, so I went on. <Anyway, where are the other two?>

<Who? Estrella and Spectre? You don't have to worry about them. They're at the hospital.>

<Hospital?>

<Yeah. You bopped Spectre on the noggin pretty hard. Estrella teleported him there and hasn't left his side - even though Gray has been ordering her to come after you again.>

<Wow. I wouldn't have expected a merc like her to be so devoted to her team.>

Rudi began broadcasting an odd emotion, a mixture of incredulity and exasperation. <You mean you don't know?>

<Know what?>

<Spectre isn't just Estrella's teammate. He's her brother.>

That was a surprise. <Are they close?>

<Very. He practically raised her.>

That explained her going bananas after he went down. Also why she was ignoring orders from Gray and sticking to Spectre's bedside.

<Well, I guess that frees me up to come after you and Josh without any problem.>

<No! Not now! After the Academy!>

<What????> I was confused again.

<You can't come for us now. You have to wait until after you come back from the Academy.>

<Why?>

<There's something you have to do there first. It won't make a difference if you get us before you go there.>

<I'm at a loss here. Have you seen something?>

<Yes, but it's not really clear. I just know you have to go to the Academy before any rescue attempt. So just forget about us for now and go do whatever you normally would - eat junk food, watch TV, whatever - and just come for us when you get back.>

<You're kidding, right? After the fight I just had, I don't think I can go back to my normal routine. It's clear that Gray is after me now. I may not even make it to the Academy if he sends someone else.>

<No, it'll be fine. You leave for the Academy tomorrow, and I caught a glimpse of Gray's next few days just before you came back.>

<And...?>

<And that debacle in the Louvre will keep him busy for the better part of a week. Leaving his card on

Blitz will implicate him - people in certain circles will know how to trace it back to its origin - and he'll spend the next couple of days fighting for his political life. In an hour, you'll be a low priority - at least for a few days.>

<And you're sure about this? About waiting to get you and your brother?>

<Yes, we'll be fine. It's what you do at the Academy that will be important. Just don't forget about us when you come back.>

<I won't; I promise.>

<Good. I trust you.> There was a slight hesitation, and then she spoke again. <Okay, with Estrella adamantly refusing to leave her brother, Gray has called for an abort on this mission for now. We're leaving.>

I heard an engine rev up, and then saw a white commercial van with "Benny's Electrical and Plumbing" on the side pull out of a parking spot and head towards the street running parallel to the mall. I could feel Rudi inside, getting farther away.

<Wait!> I suddenly cried out. <How will I find you?!>

<Chamomile!>

Huh?

MUTATION

Chapter 10

Most experts agree that the average streetfight lasts less than a minute. Those numbers usually have to be adjusted upwards for supers, but they were very much in line with what I'd gone through with Estrella's team. It had felt like an eternity, but the time we spent actually engaged in combat (not counting the time I spent talking to Rudi) wasn't particularly long at all - probably no more than three minutes, max.

Thus it was that, when I teleported back to my grandfather's car, less than fifteen minutes had actually passed since Gray and I had been on the phone. I then spent a few moments zipping around the garage at high speed in order to locate the car keys I'd apparently dropped when Estrella's team jumped me.

Surprisingly, mall security on an overall basis had done a better job than the individual efforts of the guards who had faced off with Estrella's group. The parking garage was shut down - no ingress or egress - until the threat inside could be fully assessed. Of course, the prior threat was currently neutralized, but I didn't bother telling them that.

Since I couldn't drive myself home, I did the next best thing: I found a secluded corner and parked. I was about to teleport myself, car and all, back home when I caught a glimpse of myself in the rearview mirror. There was a blatantly obvious bruise where Estrella had backhanded me. I also didn't doubt that there'd be a lot of discoloration around my chest and midsection as well. Moreover, with the adrenaline of the fight wearing off, I was starting to feel some acute discomfort, if not actual pain.

MUTATION

Frankly speaking, I wasn't too worried. As a shapeshifter, I wouldn't have any problem covering up bruises. In other words, I would appear to be fine aesthetically (which was great since Electra and I had a last-night-before-school-starts date set for later that evening). Subcutaneously, however, the injuries would still be there. And while I enjoyed a high metabolism that allowed for swift recuperation from most injuries, I still had to fuel that recovery through intake of the proper nutrients. In short, I needed to eat something - and a lot of it. I also needed information regarding Rudi's mysterious one-word clue as to locating her: Chamomile.

So, food and information. Hmmm…there was one person who was ideal for providing both. I picked up my phone, which was still in the car's cupholder, and called Braintrust.

****

Braintrust, whom I usually referred to as "BT," was a huge cluster of clones sharing a single hive mind. Along with my grandfather, BT had been responsible for much of my training over the years, and had had considerable influence in teaching me how to use my powers.

Historically, the BT clone who I'd dealt with had been male. Thus I had developed a habit of referring to BT as "he," even though I knew he had clones of both genders. During a crisis a few weeks back, that particular clone had been killed. (Needless to say, "killed" was a relative term with respect to BT's clones. As my grandfather had once put it, losing clones was, for BT, somewhat akin to a normal person getting a haircut.) Since then, the BT clone I'd been dealing with was a blond woman - a fact made more disconcerting by the fact that she was very attractive.

The blonde in question was waiting for me when I teleported my grandfather's car into the garage of the house she was staying in. It was a place I'd been to before - a nondescript house in a middle-class neighborhood, just a small step down from the place where my family was currently living. (In fact, BT was the friend who'd provided us with the house where Mom, Gramps, and I currently resided.)

BT was standing in the doorway that led from the garage into the house. I got out of the car and approached her, extending a hand for her to shake (something I always did with the previous BT clone). She ignored it and instead gave me a hug and a peck on the cheek. I blushed, but BT didn't seem to notice. I had completely forgotten that BT's clones are all tempered to act the same way normal individuals would in society. Thus, his female clones were apt to be less formal (which explained why I got a hug instead of a handshake).

She turned and walked into the house. I followed, passing through a small utility room housing a washer and dryer before going through another door into the kitchen. BT pointed to a nearby counter, where a loaf of bread, some prepackaged sandwich meat, a bag of chips, and a two-liter bottle of soda sat.

"Sorry," BT said, "I don't have anything prepared. I wasn't expecting you until later."

I simply nodded in acknowledgement. Ordinarily, if BT knows I'm coming, there will be a buffet laid out for me, with everything from steak to prime rib. This being my last day before heading to the Academy, I had already made plans to come by, but had shown up earlier than anticipated.

I shifted into super speed, then made and wolfed down three hearty sandwiches - along with the bag of chips and half a liter of soda - in record time. I slowed back down to normal speed after making the fourth, intending to eat it at a more leisurely pace.

"So," BT said, "you didn't give a lot of detail on the phone - just that you'd had a run-in with some people and were hungry. Care to elaborate?"

I nodded, and - between bites - brought her up to speed on the day's events.

"Well, I'll give you this much," BT said when I finished, "you definitely punch your weight. I'm not saying the rest of her team was paltry, but Estrella's a class apart."

"Really?" I was admittedly a little surprised. She had some impressive powers, but nothing I hadn't seen before (although not exactly in that combination). "What makes her so special?"

"You're kidding, right? You do know what her name means?" BT asked.

"It means 'star' in Spanish," I said, happy to have finally gotten some use out of two years of foreign language classes.

"And that's exactly what she is. She's literally a living star. So, aside from the A-Level powers such as flight, super strength, and teleportation, she's also got lasers and heat, among other things. She's the sun personified - a walking, talking fusion reactor."

"Hmmm...so how would you beat someone like that?"

"Why, are you worried she might come after you?"

I shrugged noncommittally.

"I wouldn't worry too much about it. First of all, your friend the precog said you could carry on as usual. If she's as good as you say - and you trust her - then it's almost guaranteed that Estrella won't seek you out. Even more, she's completely mercenary. Although her brother got hurt, Estrella's not coming after you unless there's a payday in it for her - presumably one separate and apart from whatever she received to come after you today. That said, I don't think she'd be above seeking a little payback if your paths happen to cross at some point. But beyond that, you should be fine."

"Still though, how would I take her down if I had to?"

"How do you beat the sun?" BT asked rhetorically, throwing her hands up in exasperation. "You can't. It just has to die on its own."

"So, stars do die, then?"

"Of course. Everything dies eventually."

"How does it happen? For stars, I mean."

"Well, stars have a dense core that results from the fusion reactions taking place inside them. When the core becomes dense enough, the star collapses under its own weight. Eventually it goes supernova - it blows up in a gigantic explosion that's brighter than an entire galaxy."

A nauseating thought suddenly occurred to me. "Is-is that what's going to happen to our sun?"

"Of course; it happens to every star." BT must have noticed the look of consternation on my face, because she went on. "Of course, that process of exploding isn't something that takes place overnight. It might take ten thousand years or more for the star to go supernova once the process begins."

I almost laughed. "So, if Estrella gets it into her head to come after me, about the only thing that can stop her is a natural process that may take ten millennia to complete."

"Essentially, yes. But while her bodily processes duplicate those in a star, she's still a human being, so the time differential for how fast the supernova process occurs might be different."

"Faster, you mean."

BT shrugged. "Might be faster, could possibly be slower."

"Great," I said sarcastically. "That's just great."

"There's also another option. As powerful as she is, I still doubt that she's a match for Alpha Prime. He could probably—"

"Forget it," I stated forcefully, cutting her off. I'd rather roast in the fires of Gehenna than ask my father for help. "Besides, this is all just theoretical. I may never even see Estrella again."

"Good point," BT noted, nodding in acquiescence.

"Now, what about Rudi and that clue she gave me - Chamomile?"

"Chamomile's a code name for a special government black ops program. It's actually an umbrella slate that encompasses a number of covert agendas, some of which relate to supers and their powers."

"Can you find out where it's located? Or more specifically, where they're holding Rudi and her brother?"

"Not a problem, but it may take some time."

MUTATION

I nodded in acknowledgement, but wasn't too worried. Information was BT's stock in trade. There was very little that he - excuse me, *she* - didn't know or couldn't find out. On top of that, she was amazingly smart - probably the smartest person I knew outside of Mouse. The thought put me in mind of Vixen's request.

Inspiration hit me like a lightning bolt, and I started telling BT about my brilliant Alpha League mentor.

MUTATION

Chapter 11

I drove straight home after leaving BT's place. Again, there was a certain excitement that came from sitting behind the wheel, and not all of it was due to the fact that I was driving without a license. Learning to drive made me feel…mature, I suppose. Like I was passing out of adolescence and entering the next phase of development - not exactly an "adult," so "young adult," I guess, would be the proper terminology.

The new clothes that I had purchased passed muster, getting a big thumbs-up from Mom. After carrying it all up to my room, I tore the tags off everything and packed it all away.

As it was my last day before leaving, I had initially thought it appropriate to spend it with my family. However, Mom and Gramps wouldn't hear of it.

"It's your last night before school begins," my grandfather had said. "You should be spending it with your friends, enjoying that last bit of freedom."

"But I won't see you and Mom for months," I'd replied. "I'll be seeing those other guys every day."

"Still," Mom had tacked on, "it'll do you some good to get out and have some fun. You don't want to start off the school year with a reputation of being a mama's boy who stayed inside on the last day of summer instead of going to play with the other kids."

In the end, we settled on a compromise: I would have an early dinner with my family, and then go out. Thus, I had eventually set up a date with Electra for later.

Dinner itself turned out to be a couple of my favorites. The main course was smothered steak with rice and gravy, followed by brownie *a la mode* for dessert.

MUTATION

Because Mom rarely ever uses her powers, the three of us usually converse verbally, but – for once – that manner of discourse was kept to a minimum as we telepathically had a very lively discussion during dinner. For instance, Gramps shared anecdotes from when Mom was a child, while she told how her stern father morphed into a pushover once a grandchild was added to the mix. As I mentioned before, though, communication between telepaths is far more than just words, and the meal ended with me feeling even closer to my mother and grandfather than usual, which is saying quite a lot.

****

Following dinner, Mom took on the task of washing the dishes, leaving me and Gramps to have some time to ourselves.

<So, what is it?> he asked when we were alone. <What's eating at you?>

At this juncture, my grandfather knew me almost as well as I knew myself, so I didn't even bother asking how he knew something was wrong. Instead, I just conveyed to him what had happened at the mall.

<So, what's the problem?> he asked when I'd finished.

<The problem is that I nearly got my ticket punched this afternoon.> I hesitated, not sure how to go on. <What if I'm not ready for this? To be a superhero?>

Mentally, my grandfather slapped his knee in laughter. <That's what you're worried about? A guy who regularly hunted super criminals to collect bounties is ready to hang up his cape the first time winning a fight takes a little bit of effort?>

MUTATION

<It was more than just a little bit of effort. Those guys were cleaning my clock! If I hadn't realized that they were using a psychic–>

<But you did. That's what makes you suitable for this. Not everybody could have figured things out and come up with a viable plan.>

<It didn't feel all that viable. At the time, it just felt like I'd been dealt a lousy hand but had no choice but to play the cards I held. I guess I'm just lucky that it all panned out.>

<Luck had nothing to do with it. That was training coupled with your innate talents – not just your powers, but also the inherent ability to think on your feet.>

When I didn't say anything, he went on.

<Nevertheless, you shouldn't feel obligated to do this. You don't have to go down this path just because I did, or your grandmother did, or…or because of anyone else. You don't have anything to prove to anybody, and I will be just as proud of you if you decide you want to be an architect, a vet, or a stand-up comedian.>

I burst out laughing at that last one. <No, there's no doubt that this is what I want to do. Who doesn't want to be a superhero? The real question is whether I'm good enough.>

He hesitated for a moment before speaking. <Listen, Jim. I wore a cape for a long time, and I worked with the best in the business, so believe me when I say that you're as good as they come. And I'm not just saying it because you're my grandson or because I had a hand in your training. I'm saying it because it's true.>

This little speech had the effect, as he probably knew, of making me feel a whole lot better.

MUTATION

<By the way,> he continued, <that thing at the Louvre was the cherry on top. Gray will have his hands full fixing that mess, but make no mistake about it, he'll be coming after you with a vengeance next time.>

I nodded in acknowledgement, but still had a warm fuzzy from my grandfather's words of encouragement.

MUTATION

Chapter 12

I spent a few more hours with Mom and Gramps - mostly playing some board games - before heading out for my date with Electra. In fact, it was to be a double date; my friend Smokescreen and his girlfriend were joining us and we were all going to a drive-in.

I arrived at the safe house about an hour early. I wanted to have a final powwow session with Mouse, and I'd also asked him to reach out to Alpha Prime so we could have a chat before I left for the Academy. The former I was looking forward to; the latter, not so much.

Mouse was hanging out in the common area when I came in, sipping what appeared to be a coffee and tapping away on a computer tablet. He barely glanced up as I sat down across from him.

"You all set?" he asked matter-of-factly.

"I suppose," I said with a shrug. "I followed the suggested list of items to bring, but it's not like I've done this before."

"Well, did you ask anybody?" He looked up, setting the tablet aside. "Electra? Smokescreen? Any of the other teens?"

"No," I answered sheepishly. "I didn't want to come across as some ignorant hick."

"Apparently the great Kid Sensation is starting to believe his own press. Look, it's not going to hurt your market value to ask some of your peers for advice. They've been to the Academy; they know the pitfalls, the things to look out for."

"I just figured I'd ask you if I had any questions. *You're* my mentor."

"Yeah - a mentor who never went to the Academy. You seem to forget that I failed the Super Teen Trials three years in a row."

"I know, but the Alpha League is now led by that three-time loser."

"Whoa, whoa, whoa! 'Three-time loser'? I don't remember planting that label on myself."

"Well, you admittedly failed three times in a row. I think that qualifies you for the title."

"The point of my previously sharing that with you," Mouse said, tapping his finger on the table for emphasis, "was not to paint my failures in broad strokes like you're doing, but to highlight the fact that there were flaws in the system used to identify talents among supers. Thus, my failures were more of an indictment of the methodology used at the time than a reflection on my abilities."

"And just what are those abilities?"

For a second there, it looked as if Mouse were about to speak, and then he laughed. "Nice try, Kid, but that's nowhere near good enough to get info from me."

I smiled, graceful in defeat. Despite being my mentor, I still didn't have a handle on what Mouse's power was. I'd tried to coax it out of him before, but he'd never say. Likewise, trying to trick him into revealing it - as I'd just attempted - typically ended in failure.

"Anyway," Mouse continued, "since you've got time to clown around, I'm just going to assume that you've got all the bases covered with respect to the Academy. And if you don't, the first two days are going to be orientation for the new people, so you can get all your questions answered then."

"Wait a minute," I said, frowning. "If rookies like me are going through orientation, what are veterans like Electra and Smokescreen going to be doing?"

"Getting re-acclimated. Reacquainting themselves with school resources like sports equipment, scouting locations for off-campus field trips such as the lake…"

"In other words, they'll be goofing off for the first couple of days while the newbies are stuck in class."

"Pretty much."

"That sounds fair."

"R-H-I-P, young man. Rank has its privileges."

"What rank? Electra and I are in the same grade!"

"But she's already been through orientation. She knows the stuff you still need to learn."

That comment reminded me of something. "Speaking of knowing things…" I went on to tell Mouse about BT and to let him know that he should expect a phone call in the next few days. Hopefully putting those two together would take some of the pressure off me with respect to Vixen's request that I do well in my classes.

I had just finished speaking when Mouse nodded in the direction behind me. "I think someone's here for you."

I turned around and saw Electra standing near the far wall. A smile started to creep onto my face - until I saw who she was talking to. Alpha Prime.

He was dressed in his Alpha League uniform. He was tall, roughly six-seven, with dark hair, chiseled good looks, and a physique that looked sculpted rather than natural. In short, unlike Rouge, he actually had the kind of appearance one expected of the world's greatest superhero. Beyond that, how do you describe power incarnate, omnipotence personified?

As I watched, he raised a hand and pointed in my direction. Electra looked in the direction indicated, then marched over to me. Behind her came Alpha Prime - walking this time, much to my surprise. Ordinarily, he would simply float from one place to the other, his primacy self-evident.

"You jerk," Electra said when she got close. I didn't have much experience with girls, but I knew that I needed to keep my mouth closed at the moment. "You're way early," she continued. "I'm nowhere near ready."

"It's okay," Mouse said. "He just popped in early to see me and AP." He nodded towards Alpha Prime. "Right, Jim?"

"Yeah," I confirmed. "You've still got plenty of time to get ready."

"Oh?" she responded. "Are you saying that I *need* a lot of time to get ready?"

"No, not at all. You tend to keep things plain, so you should be ready in practically no time."

"So now I'm *plain*? I'm just some homely, run-of-the-mill chick–"

"No, no, no," I stammered. This was going badly (although not as bad as our first date, which had ended up with Electra blasting me with a bolt of electricity). "What I meant was…"

I trailed off as I picked up on some high levels of emotions coming from around me - basically humor and mirth. I glanced around and saw Mouse and AP quietly snickering - and Electra straining not to crack a smile.

"Very funny," I said, and all three burst out laughing almost simultaneously.

"Oh man," Mouse said between chuckles, "she really had you tap dancing for a second there."

I looked at Electra and understood: this was payback for the other night at the Eiffel Tower.

"*Touché*," I said, nodding in her direction.

****

After Electra left to go finish getting ready, Mouse excused himself. Rather than talk in the common area, Alpha Prime asked that I teleport us to the roof of the safe house. Once there, he zoomed up into the sky and I followed. We leveled off at about a thousand feet. It was still light outside and we were clearly visible (should anyone be looking for a pair of guys floating up in the air), but it was as much privacy as we'd be likely to get anywhere else.

"So," he said after a moment, cape whipping behind him in the wind, "you and Electra, huh?"

I shrugged noncommittally. "I don't know. I like her, and she seems to like me."

He simply nodded, and I realized how awkward our relationship must be for him: the girl he'd helped raise almost like a daughter, and the biological son he'd barely ever laid eyes on. Not to mention the fact that we were all part of the Alpha League. It was like some weird superhero soap opera.

"She's a good girl," he said after a few moments. "I hope things work out for you guys."

"Thanks," I mumbled, caught a little off-guard at discussing my dating life.

"But as much as I want your relationship with her to work out," he went on, "I want ours - yours and mine - to work out more."

"That's why we're here," I said flatly.

"That's why *I'm* here. But you…are you here because you want to be, or because your mother made you?"

I couldn't help but crack a smile at that. "A little bit of both, I suppose. I promised her I'd try."

"You also told me a few weeks back that you were willing to work with me on having a real father-son relationship." When I didn't respond, he continued. "So what can I do?"

"Huh?" I was confused. "Do about what?"

"Tell me what I can do to get the ball rolling here."

"There's nothing to be done," I said, shaking my head in the negative.

"I know you hate me, Jim, but there's got to be something, some way I can extend an olive branch."

"I don't *hate* you," I said forcefully. "I was definitely angry for a long time, although I got to get a lot of that out of my system the last time we talked." He nodded in understanding.

"But the gist of the situation now is that I don't *need* you," I said. "There's no role for you to play. I'm practically at the age of majority, and to the extent I need a father figure, I've got Gramps. And he's always been there. Basically, we can work together and be teammates, but there's no slot for you to fit into my life outside of that."

He looked at me in an odd way, with hurt in his eyes. I could also sense pangs of anguish shooting away from him like darts, so I clamped down on my empathic ability, determined not to let sympathy for him intrude on my thoughts.

"You know," he said after an extended silence, "I haven't seen my own father since I came to this world over eighty years ago. I miss him every day, and as powerful as I am, I need him. I need his wisdom, I need his support, I need his encouragement. All men need their fathers, no matter how powerful they are."

I was tempted to say that the converse obviously wasn't true - that men apparently don't need their sons (or else he wouldn't have taken a sixteen-year hiatus from being in my life) - but something stopped me. He hadn't been a great father to me, true, but he was one of the good guys - the greatest of the good guys if you let some people tell it. And he actually was trying. Could I do any less?

I sighed in resignation. "Look, we both know this is an extremely rocky road we're trying to go down, so let's just take it in baby steps. I leave for the Academy tomorrow, but I'll be home for the holidays. Why don't you get us seats for a game or something?"

"That's months away, son," he said after a moment, and I bristled at his casual use of the word "son." "So what, we go hang out one time between now and the end of the year, then you go back to school and maybe we have another sit-down six months after that?"

"Well, I leave tomorrow. The only other options - assuming you don't pop up as a special guest at school - are to write or call, or whatever interdimensional equivalent they have for those at the Academy."

"That's fine with me. The question is, will you write or call back?"

MUTATION

I stared at him for a second with something probably akin to shock on my face. Regular and ongoing communication with my father was not something I had really anticipated. Still, I forced myself to nod stiffly.

****

We stayed aloft for a little while longer, making small talk - Alpha Prime asking about Mom and Gramps, me asking for anecdotes about Electra as a child.

When we finished speaking, I got ready to teleport us back into the safe house. Before we did, however, he surprised me by laying a hand on my shoulder.

"Look," he said. "I know I don't have a right to take pride in any of your accomplishments, but I do. Having you as my son means everything to me, and I'm immensely proud of you. And what I said before, about sons needing their fathers, is true. So just know that if you ever need me - for anything - all you have to do is ask and I'll be there. In fact, I'll be there even if you don't."

I mumbled an acknowledgement of what he'd just said, then teleported us back.

MUTATION

Chapter 13

The double date that Electra and I had with Smokescreen and his girlfriend was actually a fun time. The notion of going out together was actually Smokey's idea. He'd been on hand during the crisis a few weeks back, and while he had come through it essentially unscathed, the entire experience had given him a new outlook.

Basically, he had needed to come to grips with the fact that being a cape could actually get you killed. To be frank, I'd thought he'd reverse course and decide to live a "normal" life, so it was a bit of a pleasant surprise when he called the week before to say he'd be returning to the Academy. Then he'd asked if Electra and I would be interested in a double date.

Smokey's girlfriend, Sarah, didn't have any superpowers. That being the case, we didn't necessarily want her seeing the safe house, so Smokey – who was driving – had picked me and Electra up first. Then we had gone to get Sarah, who was a gorgeous Asian beauty with straight black hair that dropped below her shoulders.

The movie we were going to see was actually a drive-in double feature. There was a horror film and a romantic comedy – an odd combination obviously intended to attract couples.

The first movie, a dumb piece of schlock about zombies, barely held anyone's attention, so we found ourselves talking more than paying attention to the film. Sarah turned out to be both fun and witty, and – even disregarding her attractiveness – I could plainly see why any guy would be drawn to her. On my part, it was my first time at a drive-in, and I found myself thoroughly enjoying the experience (if not the movie).

When the first film ended, there was a short intermission before the second was to begin. While our dates excused themselves to go to the ladies' room, Smokey and I stepped out of the car to stretch our legs.

For a few minutes, neither of us really said anything. Empathically, I could feel something building inside him, a kind of anxiety that he was longing to let out.

"I'm glad you decided to come back to the Academy," I finally said. "It'll be nice to have one person I know already there."

"You don't have to worry about knowing anyone," he replied. "Everybody already knows you – the intrepid Kid Sensation."

I frowned a little. The moniker of "Kid Sensation" was actually a media concoction, not something I'd come up with myself. Yet I'd never bothered trying to refute the sobriquet or distance myself from it.

"That doesn't necessarily mean everyone will want to be my friend," I said.

"Like who? Your competition?" He nodded in the direction of a guy near the concession stand. I looked as directed and recognized the person in question as Dynamo, another teen with an enviable power set that included an ability I'd been longing for: super strength.

For a second, I thought it highly coincidental that Dynamo would also be here on the same night we were. Looking around, however, I quickly realized that there were quite a number of super teens here that I recognized. Then I remembered: coming to this drive-in on the last night of summer had become kind of a tradition among super teens in the area.

Still, I was a little puzzled by Smokey's comment. "What do you mean 'competition'?" As far as I knew, Dynamo – in addition to having cool powers – was also an all-around nice guy.

"Well, with Paramount gone, there's a void at the top of the pyramid. Which teen is the new golden boy who will lead the next generation of supers? Everyone is laying odds that it's either you or Dynamo."

"Why does it have to be anyone? Having all that pressure on him is part of what broke Paramount. As far as I'm concerned, the slot can stay empty."

Smokey shook his head and made a tsking sound. "You don't know much about science, do you? Nature abhors a vacuum, my friend. That spot will be filled, either willingly or unwillingly."

"Well, why don't you take it?"

"Yeah, right," he said sarcastically. "I've got an extremely low-level talent – the ability to make smoke. It took that battle we had to make me finally realize that I'll never be anything more than a sidekick at best, with only the ability to create a distraction in the field."

"What are you talking about? You helped save the world! Regardless of talent level, that means something."

"I barely did anything," he retorted. "It was mostly you and Mouse, and some help from Electra. I'm not sure that what I did would even count as an assist."

Understanding dawned on me in an instant. "So that's what it is. You're thinking you don't belong at the Academy, that you shouldn't be a cape."

"Let's face it, man. Ultimately, I'm probably more of a liability in the field than an asset."

"If that's the case, then what changed your mind about coming back to school?"

He was silent for a moment before answering. "I didn't tell anyone the entire story, but my parents knew something had happened – just from the way I was acting. Plus, there was the whole thing with Alpha League HQ getting demolished. Basically, they told me that they didn't want me to go back. They'd rather have me alive and living 'normal' than dead and a hero. And I felt the same. So did Sarah."

"Wait a minute," I said in surprise. "You told her? You told her you're a super?"

"I had to tell her something. We've been together for three years, and for the last two – as far as she knew – I've been away at boarding school most of the time. That means the summer is really the only time we have together. But with me moping around for most of the past few weeks and shutting her out, she was getting ready to write me off. I could feel it. So I told her."

"And did it help?"

"Lots. Being aware of what I was going through let her know that the problem wasn't a lack of interest in her. She realized it was something I needed to work through and having her support meant a lot.

"So I spent a week hanging out doing what non-powered people do. Trying to figure out what I would do with my life, what kind of job would I want if I didn't have to worry about fighting super criminals, mad scientists, alien monsters…"

"Sounds kind of boring," I interjected as he trailed off.

"You would not *believe* how boring!" he shot right back, laughing.

"So basically, you're coming back because you're now an adrenaline junkie."

"I guess so," he chuckled. "So now it's just a matter of adjusting to the fact that, with my power set, I probably won't ever be more than a D-List superhero."

I put a hand on his shoulder. "Regardless of power level, I'll take you over just about anybody out there any day of the week."

He grinned. "Thanks."

****

The second movie of the double feature, the rom-com, actually seemed quite good (although I suspected it only appeared that way because the lead-in film was so terrible). Like most films in the genre, there was the silly misunderstanding between the love-struck couple, the mad dash to the airport, and the confession of love before a room full of strangers. In short, nothing really new, but that didn't keep it from being enjoyable.

Afterwards, we participated in another tradition that I was unfamiliar with: all of the super teens went to eat at a late-night grill that was owned by a couple of former superhero sidekicks. The house specialty was the chili-cheese fries, and the owners let all the teens get a free order of them in honor of it being the last day of summer for us.

"So," Sarah said while reaching for some fries, "is everyone here a super?"

"I don't know if I'd go so far as to say everyone," Electra answered, glancing around. If she was surprised that Sarah knew about us, she didn't show it visibly or emotionally. "But most of them definitely are."

"It just seems weird to me, knowing that someday, probably in the near future, some of these people are going to be saving the world – along with my Sugarbear." She patted Smokey on the cheek and gave him a light peck on the lips.

"Sugarbear?" Electra and I said in unison.

"Shut up," Smokey said, glaring at both of us as Electra and I started laughing.

"So what exactly did, uh, Sugarbear tell you about supers?" I asked when I finally caught my breath again.

"Not much. Just that he goes to the Academy. And that he plans to regularly put his life in danger."

"And you don't like it," Electra stated.

"At first, no, I didn't. I wanted him to quit. I know we're just kids and it's not like we're going to get married or anything, but he's a good guy. I didn't like the idea of him getting hurt. Plus, just looking around here, it looks like there are enough future capes here to make ten superhero leagues."

"But…?" I asked when it seemed like she wasn't going to go on.

"But," she finally said, "what he's doing is important. There has to be somebody willing to put it all on the line, whether it be a superhero, a policeman, a fireman, a soldier, what have you. Because if we aren't willing to risk anything, we risk losing everything."

I nodded in agreement as she spoke, suddenly understanding why Smokey had been willing to share his deepest secrets with this incredibly insightful girl.

MUTATION

Chapter 14

The double date ended with Smokey letting me and Electra out at my house. This was an impromptu decision, made primarily because a) Smokey wanted his night to end with him alone with his date (as opposed to with me and Electra), and b) we still didn't think it wise that Sarah see the safe house. In short, the drop-off order for the double date couldn't simply be the inverse of the pick-up order. Electra and I needed to exit first; ergo, I suggested my house.

Knowing that I was going to use my teleportation power, Smokey didn't wait until we were safely inside; he simply honked his horn lightly and sped off. Once they were far enough away, I got ready to take us back to the safe house, but then I felt relief and an easing of tension coming from inside our home. Although it was getting way late, an unexpected feeling suddenly motivated me in an unsuspecting way.

I turned to Electra. "Would you like to meet my mother?"

****

There's something odd that happens when mothers and girlfriends (if Electra could be considered such) meet for the first time. There's often this little tug-of-war, an odd back-and-forth as each tries to figure the other out. Sometimes it ends disastrously, with the women hating each other. In my case, it was just the opposite, with Mom and Electra taking to each other as if they were the blood relations and I the outsider.

Mom, of course, was over the moon about meeting Electra. This was the first girl I'd ever even dated, let alone brought home, and she was determined to make her feel welcome.

Electra, on her part, seemed equally smitten. I think part of it was the fact that my introducing her to my mother was an indication that I did indeed think Electra was special.

All in all, during an introductory meeting that couldn't have lasted longer than thirty minutes, they exchanged phone numbers, shared beauty tips, agreed to write each other while Electra was at the Academy, and promised to go shopping together during the holiday break.

Shortly thereafter, I teleported Electra back to the safe house, where I received a memorable kiss before returning home. I really did like her, and it seemed odd to me that, although our date had just ended, I'd be seeing her again in a few hours when we'd be leaving for the Academy.

I took a quick shower and climbed under the sheets. Although it had been a long day, I didn't feel particularly tired. I closed my eyes anyway, trying to force sleep to come.

I'd only been lying there for a few minutes when the hinges on my door squeaked softly. I didn't have to open my eyes to know that it was my mother; I could feel the emotions flowing out from her as she came into my room: love, affection, and anxiety over her only child.

To the best of my knowledge, she hadn't done this in a while – watch me while I slept. When I was younger, I know that it was almost a habit with her, the need to check on me and make sure I was safe. I know a lot of guys my age would have hated it, would say it made them feel like a baby, but it didn't bother me in the least. In fact, if it made my mother feel better, then I was all for it.

I felt her place her hand on my head, then touch my face the way she would when I was small. I opened my eyes and looked at her.

"Mom, is everything alright?"

"I'm sorry," she said. "I just…I just wanted to see you one last time before you leave tomorrow."

"You'll see me in the morning. I wasn't going to slip out before you woke up."

"I know," she said, laughing and taking a seat on the edge of my bed as I sat up. "But when you're asleep, I remember the way it used to be when you were small. When you needed me. Now you're practically all grown up – bringing girls home, heading off to the Academy – but for a second I could pretend you were still my little boy."

"It's not like I'm going to be gone forever. I'll be home for the holidays and summer, and the rest of the time I can write and call."

"Yes, but it'll be different. You've had your powers for a while, but after this, you'll really be recognized as a superhero – and one of the elite ones at that."

There was a slight trembling in her voice as she spoke. I had a sudden idea of where this was all coming from. We never really talked about it, but if there was ever a time to do so, it was now.

"Do you miss it?" I asked. "Being a superhero?"

She snorted derisively. "What's to miss? I was a cape for all of two seconds. People barely remember me.

I had hoped to make an impact, but then–" She sniffed slightly before continuing. "Then your father and I…before I knew it you were en route, and being a superhero didn't seem like a viable option any more. So I turned to my other passion – writing romances. And trying to be a good mother."

"I'm sorry, Mom," I muttered, eyes downcast. Below her maternal feelings for me, I could sense a slight amount of anguish, a small sense of loss over what might have been.

"Hey!" she uttered forcefully, taking my chin in her hand and lifting it until I met her eyes. "Don't you ever be sorry – for anything! You've done nothing wrong. I may not have gotten my own personal happily-ever-after, but I got you. And you are worth a thousand happy endings. Don't ever doubt that or forget it."

With that, she kissed me on my forehead and left, closing the door behind her.

MUTATION

Chapter 15

Morning came with exceptional swiftness from my point of view. It seemed like I had barely drifted off before Gramps was banging on my door, telling me to get up.

I got dressed quickly, then went downstairs where Mom had made bacon, eggs, and toast for breakfast. Not wanting to prolong things, I raced through the meal almost at super speed. Then it was time to go.

We had already made the decision that we would say our goodbyes at home. I didn't want Mom bawling in front of a bunch of strangers, and I was still wary of people knowing my superhero lineage. Even Mouse didn't know that my maternal grandparents were supers; he only knew that Alpha Prime was my father.

Bags in hand, I got ready to leave. As I suspected, Mom cried, but at least they were silent tears. Gramps wasn't particularly sympathetic.

"Geez, Geneva," he said. "You act like we're never going to see the boy again. He'll be home again before you know it."

"And at that point," I added, "you'll be so used to me being gone and having a life again that you won't want me back for long."

Mom didn't really say anything, but she didn't have to. There was an outpouring of emotion from her that I couldn't help but sense. And, despite his stoic demeanor, the same was true of Gramps. I felt him exuding love, pride, and warmth, as well as melancholy that I realized was sadness at my departure. I hugged them both, promised that I would write and call, then teleported.

MUTATION

****

The Academy, as I mentioned before, actually resides in another dimension, on a parallel Earth (albeit one without sentient life). That being the case, there were at least two ways to get there: magic and technology.

The only person I'd encountered thus far with enough mystical power to make the journey was Rune, the enigmatic sorcerer who was the current magic-wielding member of the Alpha League. However, he was off-planet at the moment, meaning that technology was the method of travel we'd be employing this time.

Based on my own experience, I knew that it was possible to create an aerial vortex that planes could fly through in order to get to the Academy. Today, however, we would be going through a ground-based dimensional doorway.

The departure point was a huge barn on what was – to my amazement – a working farm located about an hour outside the city limits. In all honesty, I was completely surprised when, a week before I was to leave, Mouse had given me instructions on how to get to the farm in question. On my last trip to the Academy, I'd had to travel to a secret departure point in a car with tinted windows that you couldn't see out of, then board a plane that flew into the vortex.

"That's because you were essentially a civilian back then," Mouse had said when I mentioned it to him. "Now you're officially part of the team, so we can share some things with you."

"Well, why won't we be taking a plane?" I'd asked.

"Because," Mouse had explained patiently, "when we first started opening up these dimensional rifts, they ate up a lot of power due to the fact that we were punching a hole all the way through from this side alone. Now we have equipment on both sides, so it doesn't take nearly as much power, but the machines have to be aligned, and it's the nuances of that alignment which determine whether we should open an aerial vortex, one on the ground, or elsewhere."

Thus it was that I teleported out to the aforementioned farm shortly before it was time to leave. I actually showed up behind the barn in an attempt not to startle anyone, as some people have had a bad reaction to me simply popping up out of nowhere.

As I entered the barn, I noticed that everyone else – about eighty other teens – was already inside. Almost all of them, I noticed, had at least two pieces of luggage, including Electra and Smokey, who were standing near the rear of the group. With my single duffle bag, I suddenly felt woefully unprepared, as if I'd missed some important office memo. I don't know if she sensed me or not, but Electra immediately turned in my direction as I entered.

"Where'd you come from?" she asked when I got close.

"I teleported," I answered, thinking it was an odd question since she knew my power set.

"No, I mean how'd you know how to get here?"

Now I saw what she was getting it. As far as she knew, I hadn't been here or seen the place before, so it shouldn't have been possible for me to teleport here.

"Mouse gave me directions last week. I zipped out here at super speed days ago to eyeball the place."

"Figures," she said.

Everyone was, of course, eager to get the trip underway. Before we could leave, however, we had to get a farewell speech from Buzz, the speedster who was the on-duty Alpha League member overseeing our departure. Thankfully, his remarks were brief (essentially of the do-your-best-and-study-hard variety), and then he gave the green light for us to depart.

The dimensional doorway was basically a metal ring about ten feet in diameter that was set against one wall of the barn. Various wires, tubes, and cables ran from the ring to assorted terminals and machinery that were all being operated by security guards seemingly cut from the same cloth as those manning the entrance to the safe house.

The interior of the metal ring began to shine, becoming so bright and intense that it was almost impossible to look at. At the same time, a peculiar humming noise began to fill the air.

At this point, most of the other teens pulled out sunglasses and put them on. Suddenly, I remembered Mouse's advice to ask Smokey and Electra about what to expect. Failing to do so had obviously been a rookie mistake on my part. Nevertheless, I could fix this.

I switched my vision over to another wavelength, one where the light was less intense. I smiled to myself.

Sunglasses? We don't need no stinking sunglasses!

At that point, people began to amble through the ring, bags in hand, like Third-World refugees fleeing a war-torn country. Since we were at the back of the crowd, Smokey, Electra, and I would actually be part of the last group to enter the vortex. We'd only taken a few steps forward, Electra walking immediately to my left, when I felt someone smack me - lightly but firmly - on the back of the head. I jerked around in anger and saw Smokey behind me. He tilted his head towards Electra, as if trying to tell me something. Unsure of what he was trying to get me to notice, I looked at her, but didn't see anything unusual. She was walking along with a large, fully-stuffed gym bag hanging off her right shoulder and was pulling a wheeled upright suitcase with her left hand. I looked back at Smokey and shrugged my shoulders in an I-don't-know-what-you-mean gesture. At that point, he tapped his own carry-on bag, and my eyes went wide as realization hit me.

"Let me get that for you," I said to Electra, reaching over to take the gym bag from her. I swung my own duffle bag up to my right shoulder, and then switched her bag to my right hand.

"Why, thank you," she said with a smile, and then she reached over to take my hand. I looked back at Smokey, who – even with sunglasses on – gave me a what-would-you-do-without-me look. Then we were in the vortex.

From the inside, the dimensional gateway had the appearance of a tube – an elongated cylinder of light that sparkled with various colors. At the same time, though, it was transparent, allowing me to look outside at a void so dark and endless that it boggled the mind, but which also seemed to be moving in some way, as if it might even be alive. All in all, the entire view was mesmerizing.

"Wow…" I said in complete fascination. "Do you see that?"

"See what?" asked Smokey.

"The light's too bright," said Electra in agreement. "Even with the sunglasses, I can barely see anything."

I was about to explain how the vortex appeared to me, when I noticed what appeared to be a small glowing string off to one side in the void. There was something weird about it, something other than the fact that it just didn't seem to belong out there in the opaque and murky gloom. It seemed like it was almost close enough to touch, but the darkness was so complete and encompassing, so lacking in reference points, that the object I was seeing could be ten feet away or ten miles. I telescoped my vision to get a better look at the thing in the void. When I gained a clear view of the object, I was so stunned that I almost stopped walking.

It was another vortex tube. Even more, there were people inside it. Like the teens in our own tube, the people in the other tube – primarily men – wore dark goggles. They seemed to be in the process of moving an inordinate number of machines and equipment from one side of the tube to the other.

"Well, I'll be…" I muttered.

"Jim." Electra stopped and put her hand up to shield her eyes, trying to see what I was looking at. "What is it?"

I just laughed before responding. "You wouldn't believe me if I told you."

I walked on absentmindedly, more intent on watching the people in the other tube. The angle I had wasn't great, but I could see that the end of the tube they were heading out of seemed to open in a large area like a warehouse. I also caught a glimpse of a tarp of some type covering some equipment and some letters, *A-K-A*, painted on a window with broken glass.

And then we stepped out of the vortex.

"I'm glad that's over with," said Smokey. "I always hate having to walk through."

"Me, too," agreed Electra.

They were probably waiting for me to add to their complaints about the tunnel, but I was still fascinated by what I had seen. There were other people – other worlds – making use of transdimensional technology. I didn't know what it all meant - or if it meant anything at all - but I still found it exciting.

MUTATION

Chapter 16

Unfortunately, I didn't have a lot of time to dwell on what I'd seen in the vortex. Upon arrival at the Academy, we were quickly shuffled out of the room with the vortex gate; apparently other groups would be coming through from various locations all day. Afterwards, I was immediately caught up in the hustle and bustle of registration: room assignment, class schedule, book list, etc. The only good news was that the first day was merely for settling in; orientation wouldn't begin until the following morning.

Thus it was that, a few hours after arriving, I finally found my way into my dorm room. It was a relatively spacious design – about twelve-by-twelve – with a full-sized bed, a dresser and mirror, a desk, bookshelves, and its own bathroom. There was also a good-sized closet and a couple of chairs. All in all, I felt like I'd be fairly comfortable here.

I shifted into super speed. Within a minute, I had my bags completely unpacked and everything in its proper place: clothes in the dresser drawers, toiletries in the bathroom, etc. I glanced around to see if there was anything I'd missed, and for the first time took note of the window, which sat on the wall opposite the door. It was roughly three-by-five feet in size and provided a view of the back side of the dorm, where I saw a well-kept lawn and a wooded area bisected by jogging trails.

Off in the distance, I could see other buildings, and I remembered that the actual campus was the size of a small city. Moreover, for training purposes, different areas had been designed as replicas of real-world locations. In other words, there were parts of the campus designed to look like residential areas, others built along the lines of business and commercial centers, and so on.

A dull ringing noise interrupted my reverie. I looked around and noticed the charger for a cordless phone on the desk, but no phone. The sound seemed to be coming from the top desk drawer. I opened it, and sure enough there was the phone. I took it out of the drawer and tapped the "Talk" button.

"Hello?" I said.

"Are you settled in?" asked an unfamiliar voice. I was slightly taken aback. The only two people I really knew here were Smokey and Electra. I couldn't imagine why anyone else would be calling me.

"Hello?" said the unmistakably male voice when I didn't respond. "Are you there?"

"I think you may have the wrong room," I said.

"You're Kid Sensation, right?"

"Uh, yeah."

"Then it's the right room. So again, are you settled in yet?"

"I'm, uh, I'm unpacked, if that's what you mean."

"That's good enough. I'll be there in a minute."

The line went dead; I placed the phone in the charger.

Who the heck was that?

Oh well, I would find out momentarily, I suppose. In the meantime, it occurred to me that I should check the other desk drawers in case there were other essential items hidden. Fortunately, I didn't come across anything more than some pens and pencils, as well as a pad of paper that I placed on top of the desk. At that point, someone gave a shave-and-a-haircut knock on my door. I stepped over and opened it, not sure what I'd find on the other side.

The guy standing outside my room was about my age, with short blond hair and blue eyes. He was about an inch taller than me, which would make him roughly six-one, and had a nose that had obviously been broken at some point and not set completely right. But rather than be an impediment, the nose actually seemed to give him character. That said, I would soon come to find out that he had enough character of his own.

The guy didn't wait for an invitation, but rather leaned past me and stepped into the room. He looked around the place like a drill sergeant inspecting the barracks.

"No posters on the walls," he noted, "no books on the shelves, no girlfriend's photo. Dude, I thought you said you were settled in; the place looks just like it did before you got here."

"I'm sorry," I said in confusion. "Who are you?"

"My bad, man." He extended a hand to me. "Adam Adam."

"Adam Adam?" I repeated, shaking his hand.

"Adam *Adam*," he intoned, stressing the last name. I gave him a perplexed look, indicating that I hadn't noticed the distinction in his pronunciation and my own.

He sighed in exasperation, then reached over to the notepad on the desk and tore off a sheet of paper. He held the piece of paper up at chest level, then stated his named a third time. Almost immediately, there was a popping sound, repetitive and distinct, like someone going to town on a roll of Bubble Wrap. At the same time, bits of paper shot out of the sheet he held in perfect sync with the popping noise.

After a few seconds, the noise ceased. My guest held the sheet of paper out to me. Looking at it, I saw that the bits of paper that had come out of the sheet hadn't done so randomly – they actually formed letters:

A-D-A-M-A-T-O-M

Then it hit me.

"Adam *Atom*," I said.

"Pleased to meet you," he said with a grin.

****

Adam, it turned out, was my Campus Buddy - a current student who had volunteered to be paired up with a new entrant in order to show them the ropes. He had been given my contact info (phone number, room number, etc.) when he arrived.

As to powers, he apparently had the ability to split atoms, either in small (and relatively harmless) individual bursts - as he did with the sheet of paper - or in lengthy, violent chain reactions that could explode with nuclear force.

"That last part's theoretical," he had explained. "I've never actually *caused* a nuclear explosion, but all the experts agree that I could if I wanted to. Also, I can only make non-living atoms explode."

Outside of that, I quickly came to understand two things about Adam. First of all, he was a fantastic Campus Buddy. He had a thorough knowledge of where everything was located at the Academy, and with him leading the way I quickly found out where all my classes were located, where each portion of the new student orientation was to take place, and where to pick up my supplies - books, uniforms, and so on.

The other thing I discovered about Adam is that he had a well-deserved reputation as a practical joker. One of his favorites seemed to be making someone's pen explode so that they got ink on themselves and everything else. (That one, however, usually involved Adam receiving a cleaning bill, so he didn't pull it too often.) He didn't stop there, though. If you tried slipping someone a note during a class that he was in, you might find it exploding into confetti in your hands. Or if you were drinking a soda, you might suddenly find it leaking through a small hole in the bottom of the can.

After discovering all this from Adam himself, I should have realized that I wouldn't have immunity from his sense of humor, and I didn't. Thankfully, he didn't play his first - and last - joke on me until later in the afternoon.

We had just finished taking my supplies back to my room, and I was congratulating myself on getting everything done early enough that I would have a bit of free time. That's when Adam suggested a late lunch.

A few years back, I'd participated in the Super Teen tryouts, and the Academy was the place where part of my testing had occurred. I had also visited as recently as a few weeks ago as part of a program to help teens with super abilities develop a network and camaraderie. Thus, I already knew where some facilities were, including the cafeteria.

Despite the fact that it was late afternoon, there were a fair number of people in the lunch line. Presumably, this was because quite a few had been going through the same ordeal I had earlier in terms of preparing for orientation and school. Still, the line moved fairly swiftly, and before we knew it we were through and headed towards an empty table to sit down and eat.

I had gotten a burger and fries, as well as a soft drink that came in a disposable cup with a plastic top. I had also picked up a drinking straw, still factory-wrapped in paper, and was preparing to take it out and place it in my soda when it unexpectedly exploded in my face, showering me with confetti.

"I'm sorry, man. I couldn't resist," said Adam, laughing - as were the kids at the table next to us. "Here, you can have my straw. I picked up an extra." He held a straw out to me.

I nodded but didn't say anything as I took a hand and wiped the bits of paper from my face before reaching for the straw he offered. This time when I unwrapped it nothing happened, but when I tried to put it in my soda the plastic top exploded. It startled me slightly, making me slosh the soda around and get some on my hand. Adam laughed hysterically.

There was a napkin holder on the table, and I reached for one to dry my hand. No sooner had I pulled it out than it burst into a jillion pieces. Adam almost fell out of his chair laughing.

That was it. I'm an easygoing fellow and like a good laugh as much as the next person, but I didn't have the patience to deal with this. I teleported him, sending him over by the food line. He was in a sitting position when I sent him off, but I didn't send the chair with him. The end result was that when he appeared, he immediately flopped down onto his butt. Laughter broke instantaneously, as kids throughout the room pointed and giggled.

MUTATION

For a second, Adam looked disoriented - as if he didn't know what had happened (which he quite possibly didn't). Then he noticed everyone laughing all around him. Laughing *at* him. His brow furrowed; for once in his life he was the butt of the joke, and he didn't seem to care for it.

Adam got up, dusted himself off, and headed back to our table. He smiled gleefully at everyone chuckling all around him, trying to make it clear that he could take a joke.

"That was a good one," he said when he got close. He placed his hands on the table and prepared to sit. "You really got–"

I teleported him again as he was in the process of sitting, cutting him off.

Next to the cafeteria was the student break room. It was filled with all kinds of games - pool tables, air hockey, table tennis, etc. - and during the school year it was usually full of students. I'd popped Adam in there this time.

Uproarious laughter suddenly sounded from next door. I could only assume that Adam - teleported as he was preparing to take his seat - had once again ended up on the ground.

A minute later he came back into the cafeteria, looking around sheepishly. I didn't say anything as he approached; I just kept eating my lunch.

"Well, that was fun," he said when he got to the table. "People think I love a good practical joke, but you've got me b–"

I teleported him again - this time to the jogging trail I had seen outside the window of my room. As before, he was in the process of sitting when it happened, so I assume he went sprawling in the dirt. It was a full ten minutes before he made his way back to the cafeteria.

Instead of approaching me directly, he grabbed a white napkin from a table near the door and walked over, waving it in the air.

"Truce, truce," he said as he approached. He placed the napkin on the table when he got close enough. Then - very carefully and looking me in the eye the entire time - he took his seat.

Thereafter, I had no more issues with Adam or his practical jokes.

MUTATION

Chapter 17

After lunch there was nothing formal on my agenda until orientation the next day. I was supposed to meet Electra and Smokey a little later, but at present I wanted to explore.

From a teleportation standpoint, my strength lies in being able to send various items (including myself) to any one of numerous locations. Thus, the more places I visually log into my teleportation rolodex, the more options I have when using that power. With respect to the Academy, this meant I needed to see as much of the place as possible.

Once he understood what I was hoping to do, Adam was an impressive tour guide. He not only took me to all of the major spots on the campus map - the library, the gymnasium, the commissary (where I bought an entire box of candy bars) - but he also showed me several lesser-known but good-to-know-about areas: rarely used stairwells, isolated areas of the mazelike basement, sparsely utilized entrances and exits, etc.

By the time we finished (at a door that led down to a sub-basement level), I only had about an hour before I was to rendezvous with Smokey and Electra in the break room. I gave Adam a breakdown of our plans and told him that he was free to join us, then teleported back to my room.

I tossed my box of candy bars on the dresser, then looked around the room. The supplies I had picked up earlier were sitting on my bed, which is where I'd tossed them when Adam and I had made a pit stop here earlier before heading to lunch.

MUTATION

I switched into super speed, then began putting up the supplies I'd received: books on the shelves, uniforms in the closet, and so on. I'd even been issued a laptop, which I set up and connected in no time flat. As before, it took me less than a minute to get everything done.

When I finished, I grabbed one of the candy bars, ripped it open, and began eating it. I hadn't used up an inordinate amount of energy at any point today, but I typically liked to eat something after shifting my metabolism into high gear. Better safe than sorry.

Afterwards, I stretched out on the bed, relaxing for the first time that day it seemed. Everything was still somewhat surreal to me. I was actually here - at the Academy! - officially about to start fulfilling my dream of becoming a superhero. Of course, it was coming a couple of years after I had originally passed the requisite tests, but I was here all the same. Better late than never.

At the same time, my mind turned back to what I had observed in the vortex. I couldn't stop thinking about the other people I'd seen. Who were they? What were they doing? Were they more advanced than us?

The questions I asked myself came in rapid-fire fashion, and I found myself coming up with all kind of fantastic scenarios as to who those other vortex travelers might be and what their purpose was.

****

I awoke to the sound of the phone ringing, and for a second I was totally confused by the unfamiliar surroundings. Then it hit me as to where I was.

I must have been more tired than I realized. I had obviously dozed off and taken a cat nap without even intending to. I got up and reached for the phone, answering it on the third ring.

"Hello?" I said, sounding sleepier than I felt.

"Hello yourself," Electra said, her voice holding something of an edge. "Did you forget about meeting us?"

There was a clock on the desk; I was supposed to have met Electra and Smokey more than thirty minutes ago.

"Sorry," I mumbled. "I dozed off. I'll be there in a sec."

I hung up the phone and stepped into the bathroom. I spent a few minutes washing up, including splashing some cold water on my face to chase away the last bit of drowsiness. After checking the mirror to make sure I was presentable, I teleported down to the break area.

To my surprise, the room was packed - standing room only. In fact, there was also a crowd of people milling about not just outside the room but all the way down the hallway. The indecipherable chatter of hundreds of conversations going on simultaneously filled the air.

I scanned the room quickly and saw Electra and Smokey, as well as Adam, huddled up around a pool table and holding cue sticks. I walked over to them as quickly as I could without shifting into super speed. They finally noticed me making my way through the crowd when I was a few feet away.

"I'm glad you could join us," I shouted to Adam over the din, clapping him on the back.

"No problem," he said. "I'll take any opportunity to beat Electra."

I was a little surprised. "You two know each other?"

Electra laughed before responding. "The school's not *that* big, Jim. Plus, Adam and I have history."

I raised an eyebrow quizzically, and Adam offered an explanation.

"She got wind that I was going to do my exploding pen trick on her, so she decided to beat me to the punch. We had a science class together, so she went in one night and jury-rigged some gizmo to my chair so that my seat would hold an electrical charge. Then, the next day - just before I sat down - she zapped it."

Electra burst out laughing at this point. "He practically jumped through the ceiling!" she said between hysterical giggles.

"Yes," Adam replied with a sly smile. "So I still owe her an exploding pen."

Following that, we broke off into teams and played three games of pool. After each game, we switched partners so that each of us had a chance to team up with (as well as play against) everyone else.

Surprisingly, Electra turned out to be the hustler among us. She barely missed a shot, with the result being that she won every game. (The rest of us, being partnered with her only once through the course of play, won one game each.) After the third game, we gave up the table, giving other people a chance to play.

I discovered to my lament that the nap I'd taken had caused me to sleep through dinner, so I got a bunch of snacks from a vending machine and then we all went outside. It was just starting to get dark, with the stars

129

slowly becoming visible. It was still hard to believe that we were in an entirely different dimension when so much seemed the same.

We were in the main courtyard of the school. There were tons of other students out here as well, but with so much space, everyone was spread further out, giving the impression of there being fewer people in the area. We found a few unoccupied square feet of grass and sat down, and spent the next couple of hours talking (although much of it consisted of them enlightening me with regards to what to expect during my time at the Academy).

After picking their brains (and getting a full list of rookie mistakes to avoid - like missing dinner - while I munched on snacks), I noticed students starting to drift inside. As it was getting close to curfew, we decided to follow suit, with Smokey and Adam heading off to the guys' dorm and me walking Electra to hers.

The guys' and girls' dorms were actually at opposite ends of the main campus. (What's up with that?) Furthermore, there was a lobby/common area on the ground floor of each dorm that members of the opposite sex were not allowed to go beyond.

In brief, Electra and I found ourselves saying goodnight in the lobby of her dorm, along with dozens of other couples. Moreover, there was a staff member - a matronly woman with a stern and unforgiving look - on duty behind the lobby's main desk to make sure nobody got any ideas about sneaking upstairs.

Needless to say, none of this set the end-of the-night tone I was hoping for, so I had to settle for a quick peck on the lips, then watch as Electra slipped upstairs.

MUTATION

Chapter 18

The next few days flew by. The first two, of course, consisted of the much-maligned orientation that we newbies had heard about. It essentially boiled down to what the principal - a former super named Magnavolt - called the "Three P's": Punctuality, Performance, and Persistence. (Basically, be on time, always do your best, and always strive to improve.)

We were also informed of how communications with Earth would occur. Basically, for one hour every week, the vortex tunnel would be open. This was primarily for getting essentials for the school - food, supplies, and so on - but for students it was the only time when the communications interface would be made available for our use, allowing us to call home via special phones that had to be checked out for sixty-minute intervals. If you missed that one-hour window, you had to wait another week to make your call. (It was also when mail and packages would go back and forth, so any letters going home needed to be in the mail stack by then or - as with phone calls - you'd have to wait another seven days.)

The only other thing really hammered into us concerned the use of our powers. In essence, we could use our powers at school - which was expected, since we were here to learn to be superheroes - but any use of them outside of training that resulted in harm or damage to other students, staff, faculty, or property could subject the individual in question to suspension. That made me wonder how Adam got away with his practical jokes, but I decided that this was probably one of those rules was not heavily enforced - or, more likely, there was an unwritten rule among the students about not ratting out your fellow pupils.

The two days of orientation were followed by the weekend, so those like me who were new to the school got one last taste of freedom before classes were to actually begin. For returning students like Electra, however, not being required to go to orientation meant that they had four days off, as Mouse and I had previously discussed. However, their presence at school probably was necessary, as it got them acclimated to a structured environment once again: getting up by a certain time (unless they didn't want breakfast), figuring out their schedules so they could see if facilities or classes had been relocated, adhering to curfew, etc.

Although Electra and I were able to squeeze in some alone time for talking and several long walks holding hands, the majority of our weekend was spent with Smokey and Adam, who, I noticed, didn't seem to have a lot of close friends.

"It's his practical jokes," Electra had told me when I asked her about it. "They tend to alienate people. I'm surprised he hasn't pulled one on you yet."

I didn't bother telling her about what happened at lunch that first day, but what she told me gave me some insight into the group dynamics here at the Academy.

After the weekend, a certain melancholy seemed to settle over the student body as classes began. I can't speak for anyone else, but in my case there was adequate reason for much wailing and gnashing of teeth: the course load Mouse had chosen for me was going to be a rigorous, fast-paced affair. Just looking at the course syllabi made me want to scream, and by the end of the second day I felt my head was going to burst with everything the instructors were trying to cram in it.

The lone bright spot of the week came on Wednesday, when we got a chance to do combat training as the last class of the day.

There were actually several combat areas located around the school. The most sophisticated one used holograms. For my first day, however, I was sent to a different facility, which utilized robots that looked like crash-test dummies as stand-ins for supervillains.

Without bragging, the combat was a cakewalk for me. I'd already had years of training under Gramps and BT, so to a certain extent I was a veteran with respect to exercises like this. So, if required to put the "villain" in a certain area, I just teleported him; if I had to disarm him, I did so telekinetically; if I had to sneak past someone, I simply turned invisible.

In short, I aced every round of combat they presented to me. Of course, this first day was really meant to be more of an assessment for the new people as opposed to seeing how we'd do when things got hot and heavy. Regardless, the training instructor declared in disgust this level was too easy for me and that he was bumping me up to the holographic combat arena for the next week.

I left the combat area a little full of myself, with my head so far in the clouds that I almost bumped into Adam, who appeared almost out of nowhere and fell into step beside me.

"Where'd you come from?" I asked, still heading towards the exit from this part of the building.

"Upstairs," he said, pointing at a stairwell I hadn't noticed before. "Observation booth."

133

"There's an observation booth?" I asked in surprise.

"Of course, and it was a full house. Everybody wanted to see how the great Kid Sensation would do. And, of course, I knew there'd be some betting action on your performance, and I wanted to get in on it."

"So, how'd you make out?"

He shrugged. "I lost fifty bucks betting against you."

I laughed, and gave him a playful punch on the arm as we stepped out the door.

And there was the principal, Magnavolt.

"Jim, I need you to come with me," he said. Then he turned and walked away without waiting to see if I'd follow.

I looked at Adam, who shrugged, and then I took off after the principal. Adam, keenly interested in what was going on, came with me.

Magnavolt wasn't particularly tall but he had a long stride, so he stepped through the hallways at a fast clip. Not only his emotions (which I was picking up) but also his body language radiated tension, indicating that whatever was happening was important.

My immediate thought was that something had happened to Mom or Gramps - or worse, both. But Mom was supposed to be at a writer's convention, and Gramps should be on a fishing trip with some old cape buddies. Neither of them had said anything before I left, but I'd picked up on the fact that things at home were going to be a little quiet without me, and so both had looked for ways to occupy the time.

After a few minutes of high-stepping through the hallways, we reached the Academy's administrative wing, which housed the principal's office, teacher's lounge, and a few other areas. We marched straight in, right past the receptionist on duty and into Magnavolt's office. Once there, he directed us to a connecting conference room. Lights, obviously motion-activated, came on automatically as we entered, and I saw several executive chairs positioned around a nice-sized, rectangular conference table. However, Magnavolt didn't take a seat, so Adam and I followed his lead.

"Okay, we're here," Magnavolt said, seemingly to no one in particular. I looked in the direction where he seemed to be staring, and noticed what appeared to be a large flat screen monitor - at least fifty inches - mounted on the wall. The screen was actually split in two; on the left side was Mouse (seemingly sitting at a worktable in his lab), and on the right were two men seated at a desk. One of them I'd never seen before. He was wearing a dark blazer with a white shirt and earth-tone tie. He was rather thin, wore glasses, and was practically bald on top of his head, although he still had a fair amount of brown hair on the sides and presumably at the back.

All in all, he fit the stereotypical appearance of a weaselly, government bureaucrat.

The man seated next to him was someone I immediately recognized. It was Schaefer. He sat there, staring at me with a blank expression.

"Jim Carrow?" asked the man in the blazer, looking from me to Adam.

"Right here," I said, raising my hand, a little surprised to be the subject of an interdimensional phone conference.

"I'm Morgan Pace," he said. "I have a warrant to take you into custody. It's been delivered to your principal" –at this point Magnavolt handed me a sheaf of papers I didn't even know he'd been holding– "who has verified its authenticity and confirmed its authority."

I quickly skimmed what had been handed to me, trying to pull out the important parts while Adam read over my shoulder:

By the authority vested in me by this nation and its Constitution…as a federal judge…hereby authorize…take into custody…wherever found in our borders…

I heard Adam speak up as I continued perusing the document. "Don't you have to inform his parents of what you're doing? He *is* still a minor."

"And who are you?" Pace asked.

"Legal counsel," Adam replied, ever the jokester.

Pace harrumphed, clearly unsure of whether to take Adam seriously or not, but then said, "We attempted to reach his mother and grandfather, but were unsuccessful."

I thought about Mom and Gramps, both ironically unavailable with something like this taking place.

"However," Pace continued, "we did the next best thing. Magnavolt is principal at the Academy, so he legally has guardianship of Jim Carrow's person. And out of a sense of caution we also contacted, uh" –Pace seemed to look at something on the table in front of him– "*Mouse*, his mentor." He wrinkled his nose as he said Mouse's name, as if it were a dirty word.

"This was issued last week," Mouse said, looking at what was apparently a copy of the warrant.

"Yes," Pace said, steepling his fingers and leaning forward, "and we actually sent a team to apprehend the subject, but he resisted."

"That's not exactly true," I said, as Mouse looked at me in alarm. "They just showed up and started with the fisticuffs. They never presented a warrant."

Pace opened up his hands in a noncommittal gesture. "It's true that some of our agents have a tendency to get a little overzealous, so maybe they did overlook that tiny detail. But that would be nothing more than a technicality."

In other words, Estrella and her crew liked to brawl. That certainly explains why they decided to take on the security guards at the mall as opposed to Estrella simply teleporting them to an out-of-the-way place. Moreover, if Schaefer were involved in any way - and it now seemed likely that he was - he probably *told* them to be rough with me.

"Regardless," Pace continued, "the warrant has not yet expired, so we are asking that you return him through the vortex and hand him over to the federal government."

"I'm sorry, Jim," Magnavolt said, "but it looks like you'll have to go."

"Wait a minute!" Adam shouted. "Are you sure that thing's valid? That he's authorized to do this?"

"It's authorized," Magnavolt replied. "It's signed by a federal judge."

"So what?" Adam countered. "Can any government official just pop up with a piece of paper and take a student? What if a despot in Africa decided he wanted to get his hands on a super? Could he just send someone with a warrant? Or a dictator in the Middle

East? Would you just say 'Sorry, Jim,' and send him on his way?"

"Of course not!" Magnavolt nearly shouted. "But this is from the *government*..."

I shut out the rest of what he was saying, thinking at a maddening pace. Something Adam had said about foreign governments had given me an idea. I looked over the warrant one more time, and then made my decision.

"I'm not going," I said plainly, cutting off Magnavolt's argument with Adam. Stunned silence filled the room.

Suddenly, Pace smiled. "I'm afraid you don't have a choice. We've got the authority to take you into custody—"

"Anywhere in the nation," I finished for him. "But the thing is, we're somewhat out of the country at the moment. In fact, we aren't even on Earth as you know it. You're out of your jurisdiction."

For the first time, Pace looked unsure of himself. "Well, uh, that's, uh, that's an interesting proposition—"

"No, I'd say it's true," Adam interjected. "Principal Magnavolt just said he wouldn't just hand Jim over if a bureaucrat from some other nation just showed up with a piece of paper demanding him. Why should he do it for you?"

"That's true..." Magnavolt acknowledged softly.

For the first time since Pace had started talking, Schaefer's expression changed; he looked at Adam like he wanted to murder him.

"Mr., uh" —Pace looked down at his cheat sheet again— "uh, Mouse. My understanding is that you're a very reasonable and intelligent person. Please tell them they're wrong on this."

Mouse began gesturing and moving his lips, but no words came out. He looked around, confused.

"Looks like he lost audio," Magnavolt noted, then turned to Pace. "Regardless, this is something entirely novel - we've never had to deal with anything like this before - so until we get it sorted out, Jim stays here."

"Thank you," I said, then gave Pace and Schaefer a smug, ten-thousand-watt smile. "Adam, if you please."

I tossed the sheaf of papers into the air. Adam took his cue and a sound like tiny fireworks going off filled the air as the papers exploded into confetti and floated down to the ground.

Schaefer ground his teeth together, glaring at us.

"We'll be in touch," Pace said. His side of the screen went dark.

Adam and I were preparing to leave when I heard Mouse's voice cut through the air.

"Unbelievable," he muttered. "Even in another dimension, you somehow manage to set off a political hand grenade."

It took me a second to get over my surprise at hearing him, since his audio was supposed to be on the fritz.

"What, simply saying I wasn't going with them?" I asked.

"Yes, except it's a little more complicated - since you declared the Academy to be a sovereign nation."

"What??!!" Adam and Magnavolt sounded in unison.

"Don't you get it?" he asked them. "Jim basically said that no other nation has jurisdiction or authority there. The Academy doesn't have to obey anyone. Ergo, it's a country in and of itself - a sovereign nation."

Magnavolt's eyes went wide as saucers as the implications hit him.

"Is that why you pretended to have audio problems?" I asked.

"You betcha," Mouse said. "The last thing I needed was to get wrapped up in that kind of discussion right now. There are already factions out there who think supers - both villains *and* heroes - represent a threat. This is just going to fuel their arguments."

I was somewhat in shock. I had simply been trying to come up with a reason not to go with them, not start a secession.

"Look," Mouse said, noting the concern on my face, "it's kind of a mess, but we'll get it sorted out. Just forget about it for now and focus on school."

I simply nodded, still stunned to a certain extent.

"Oh, and by the way," Mouse added, "thanks for the intro to your friend. I think we're going to have some interesting collaborations."

For a second I didn't know what he was talking about, and then I realized he was referring to BT.

"No problem," I said. "Happy it worked out." Mouse nodded and his side of the screen went dark.

Adam and I turned and prepared to leave the room when we heard Magnavolt clear his throat in a way that clearly invited attention.

"Where do you think you're going?" he asked as we turned to him. He pointed to a mass of shredded paper on the floor - the remnants of Adam going to town on the warrant. "Clean that mess up."

We both sighed and started picking up the paper off the floor.

Chapter 19

The rest of the week passed by without incident, and by the time the weekend rolled around, I had fallen into a routine:

Wake up.

Breakfast.

Classes.

Lunch.

Classes.

Dinner.

Homework/Study.

Lights out.

Rinse and repeat.

There were only slight variations in this pattern, such as perhaps squeezing in a little time at the gym, a pick-up game of basketball, or just hanging out with Smokey and Adam.

As to Electra, we were both fairly busy so we agreed to simply try to have lunch and dinner together at least once during the week. (Naturally, we talked on the phone every night.)

All in all, I felt I had adjusted well in a short period of time. Therefore, it should have surprised no one that I was in my room getting ready for bed when someone knocked on my door just ten minutes before curfew on Friday night. I reached out empathically, quickly recognizing the emotions of the two people on the other side. I opened the door and let Smokey and Adam in.

Adam looked me up and down. I was in a t-shirt and boxers, which I normally wore to bed.

"Get some clothes on," he said. "We're going out."

"Out where?" I asked, puzzled.

"To fulfill a tradition," Adam said.

"Another tradition? It's almost curfew!" I stressed.

"And?"

I looked at Smokey for support. "Adam's right. You should get some clothes on," he said.

When I still didn't move, Adam began explaining. "Listen, after the first week of school, it's standard operating procedure for all the students to sneak out that Friday night. It started out as just a thing for lovebirds - students who were dating - but eventually branched out to everyone."

"Dude, you were in that meeting in Magnavolt's office the other day," I said. "My presence here is already controversial. I don't need to give them a reason to kick me out."

Adam was undaunted. "Point A: I recall that they told you not to worry about it, that they'd sort it out. B: nobody gets kicked out for breaking curfew. At worst, they'll just give you some punishment like detention for a week."

Again, I looked at Smokey for assistance. We had filled him and Electra in on what had happened with Pace, so none of this was news to him. However, his silence indicated that I wasn't going to get any help from his corner.

"Let's try this from another angle," Adam said. "You have a thing for Electra, right?"

I frowned. "I don't know about a 'thing,' but—"

"But you do like her?" Adam asked again.

"I guess."

"Then you'd better come."

At this point, Smokey decided to put in his two cents. "Like he said, this ritual did start off being a thing for lovebirds, so if you like someone it's tradition - and expected - that you break curfew and go meet them."

"Meet them where?"

"You'll see," Smokey replied.

****

The meeting place turned out to be a small lake about a mile from campus. You could get there via a couple of well-worn trails through the wooded area behind the guys' dorm. I had hurriedly gotten dressed and teleported the three of us outside, but that was about as far as I could take us since I initially didn't have a clue where we were going.

With the trees blocking even moonlight, the trail was exceptionally dark. I cycled my vision through the light spectrum until I could see nearly as well as in the daytime. I was sure that Adam and Smokey couldn't see nearly as well, but they seemed to know where they were going. There were odd noises coming from the brush around us, and it took me a second to realize that it was other students also slipping between the trees, headed in the same direction as us. Overhead, I occasionally heard an unexpected *whoosh*, indicating that some students were flying to the rendezvous point.

After about twenty minutes, I could see something like a light in the distance. I pointed it out to Smokey and Adam, who got excited and started to move faster. A short time later, we emerged from the

143

underbrush to find ourselves at the edge of the lake, along with hundreds of other students.

"Well, this is it," Smokey said.

I switched my vision back to normal and looked around. The light I had seen turned out to be a mid-sized bonfire, around which a number of people were making s'mores. I saw others in bathing suits, playing in the water. Another group had set up a net and were playing volleyball. All in all, there were lots of activities going on, but everyone seemed to be having fun. Moreover, tiki torches had been placed strategically around the area and were providing a more-than-adequate amount of light.

"If you're worried about the bonfire or the torches," Smokey said, "don't be. They can't be seen from campus, and the trees act as a natural acoustical barrier so sound doesn't travel very well."

"But if this is a tradition, doesn't the faculty know you're out here?" I asked.

Adam shrugged. "They do, but it's essentially harmless fun so they won't do anything unless we get out of control."

"Or if it runs too late," said a voice behind me. I turned and saw Electra, standing with two other girls.

"Hey, you," she said, giving me a wink. "Glad you could make it."

"Why didn't you tell me about this?" I asked.

"I didn't want you to feel pressured," she answered, then took my hand. "And I wanted to see if you'd find out on your own."

"Don't be rude, Electra," said one of her friends, a pale, willowy girl with hair that looked light blue in the firelight. "You should introduce us."

"Allow me," said Adam, stepping forward and extending his hand. "Adam Atom."

The girl smacked his hand away.

"Not you, clown," she said. "We already know who you are." She looked pointedly at me, as did her friend - a somewhat stout girl with red hair and freckles.

"Jim," Electra said, "This is Glacia." She indicated the blue-haired girl, who raised a cupped hand to her lips and blew on it. Snowflakes seem to fly out from her palm into the air.

I reached out to shake her hand. "How do you do?"

"And this is Sharon," she said, motioning to the redhead.

"Nice to meet you," I said.

"Come on," Electra said, tugging on my hand. "We've got a blanket spread out over here."

****

The night turned out to be an absolute blast, with fun all the way around. Sharon had brought a trivia game, so we played a few rounds of guys against the girls. Smokey, Adam, and I also got in on a couple of volleyball games. Adam even talked Glacia - who had worn a bathing suit - into going into the water with him at one point. However, something must have gone awry because she came back a few minutes later, having frozen the knee-high water he had been standing in into a block of ice. Thus, for the second time in little more than a week, the student body's most infamous prankster found himself being laughed at by everyone else.

Adam rejoined us after using his power to split the ice.

Glacia pointedly ignored him. "I'm hungry. Where's the food?"

"There's food?" I asked. Other than little snacks like s'mores and chips, I hadn't seen anything substantive to eat.

"Yeah," Smokey said. "Newbies like you don't know the ropes yet, so students returning for their *second* year have the job of bringing food."

"Well, where do we get it from?" I asked.

"Just wait," Adam said. "They'll bring it to us."

I was surprised. "They serve us?"

"They serve everybody," Electra said. "You haven't been paying attention, but they've been rolling it out for the last hour."

I frowned and glanced around. After a few seconds, I did notice people eating hotdogs and drinking from plastic cups. I also noticed that a number of students were actually running around bringing the food to everyone else.

About ten minutes later, I heard Glacia mutter, "About time." I looked in the direction that held her attention and saw a couple of guys approaching us.

The first guy was short (maybe five-four), with a cherubic face and curly blond hair. He carried a tray with hotdogs - already in buns - on it. He held the tray out to each of us in turn, and we each took one.

The other guy was slender and my height, with a Beatles haircut and glasses. He carried a drinkholder which held a half-dozen disposable cups with plastic lids (much like those in the Academy cafeteria). The straws

146

were already inserted in the cups, but still had the paper from the manufacturer on the end.

He took the cups out one by one and handed them to each of us in turn. I got mine last, and couldn't help but notice that - unlike everyone else in our group - it didn't come with a straw. Rather than raise a fuss about it, I just took the lid off and drank from the cup.

We must have all been pretty hungry, because there was almost no conversation for the next few minutes as everyone finished the impromptu meal. Smokey, Adam, and I then gathered up the cups and took them to a nearby trashcan. When we got back, the girls were folding up the blanket.

"It's getting late," Sharon said. "We should probably head in."

"Yeah," said Adam, "plus it looks like it might rain. Look at that lightning."

At that, Electra jerked her head up. "What lightning? I don't feel any lightning."

Her choice of words struck me as odd at first, and then I remembered her power. She must also be able to sense certain types of electrical discharges.

Adam pointed up into the sky. "Right there."

There was a flash of light that looked like electricity.

"That doesn't feel like lightning..." Electra said, her voice trailing off.

I telescoped my vision - and felt a mild sense of panic when I saw what was heading towards us. Or rather *who*: Magnavolt. And he was moving fast.

"Oh boy," I said. At the same time, Electra's mouth dropped open as she obviously sensed who it was as well. "We gotta move!"

147

"Incoming!!!" I shouted to no one in particular and pointed up. All heads swiveled in the direction indicated as a voice suddenly boomed out from overhead as if shouted from a bullhorn.

"WHAT ARE YOU KIDS DOING OUT PAST CURFEW???!!!"

The entire area erupted into chaos as everyone suddenly went scrambling towards the woods, trying to get away. Speedsters zipped through the trees at high speed; several flyers took to the air and zoomed away. One kid stepped into the underbrush and turned into a tree; a girl leaped into the air and shifted into a hawk. In short, teen supers were turning on everything they had, trying to keep from getting busted.

My little group wasn't immune. Aside from Electra - who only stayed put because I'd grabbed her arm - the others who had been with us scattered to the four winds like everyone else, making it impossible for me to teleport all of us. Still, if I could keep them out of trouble, I would. I teleported myself and Electra just inside the tree line - hopefully out of view of the Academy's principal but somewhat in the path of people racing back to the dorms.

On his part, Magnavolt simply floated there, calling out names.

"I SEE YOU, VANITY! BARRAGE - BE IN MY OFFICE FIRST THING MONDAY MORNING! YOU TOO, SCARAB…"

It was almost comical. In fact, when I telescoped my vision and looked at Magnavolt's face, he was actually grinning.

As I switched back to normal vision, I peripherally saw Electra reach out and grab someone trying to run past us. It was Glacia.

"Did you see any of the others?" I asked.

"No," she said, slightly out of breath, "but I think they were all ahead of me."

I looked at her skeptically. "*Sharon* was ahead of you?"

"Don't judge a book by its cover!" she retorted. "That chick is light on her feet!"

I groaned in response. We waited a few more minutes, but when we didn't see any more of our friends I teleported us back to the main building – into one of the underutilized stairwells Adam had shown me.

"Okay, we gotta go," Glacia said and started to exit the stairwell.

Electra gave me a quick smooch on the lips. "I'll see you tomorrow."

"Wait a minute," I said, grabbing her hand. "Won't you get in trouble if the faculty or staff see you? Do I need to get you guys to your rooms?"

"Don't worry about it," she said. "We won't get caught. We've been sneaking out for a long time." Then she ran to catch up with her friend.

I stood there for a moment thinking about the last thing she'd said, and wondering if I should be thankful or bothered by it. Putting it out of my mind, I teleported back to my room, took a quick shower, and hit the sack.

MUTATION

Chapter 20

I woke up the next morning drenched in sweat. My sleep had been wracked by horrific nightmares, and I had awakened screaming more than once. The worst part was that I really couldn't remember the dreams themselves – just random images, sounds, and sensations: lakes of blood, bloodcurdling screams, mounds of bodies...

I stood up - and almost swooned as the room began spinning. I massaged my temples and waited for the feeling to pass, then staggered into the bathroom. I took a towel and wiped the sweat from my face. Looking in the mirror, I saw dark circles under my eyes. Moreover, my skin looked pale and my cheeks pinched. In short, I looked like death warmed over.

But as bad as I looked, I felt even worse. My mouth felt like it was full of cotton, my stomach was doing somersaults, and my hands shook with painful spasms. Out of nowhere, I began experiencing agonizing constrictions in my chest. I started wheezing loudly as it suddenly felt like I couldn't get enough - or *any* - air in my lungs.

My training took over. I took a deep breath (or as deep a breath as I could) and held it. I focused, trying to clamp down on my body's autonomic systems and take conscious control. Slowly and deliberately, I stopped the chest constrictions, relaxing the muscles around my lungs so that they stopped trying to squeeze all of the air out of my body. Turning my attention to my stomach, I tried getting it to settle down by balancing stomach acids, altering the rate of digestion, and more. After becoming convinced that the contents of my belly were going to stay there, I concentrated on my hands, normalizing the nerves so that the tremors would cease.

When I finished, I was sweating profusely again. I turned on the faucet, splashed some water on my face and then swished some around in my mouth. I wiped my face again with a towel.

This was new territory for me. Outside of what occasionally happened when I delved into mindreading, I really couldn't recall ever being sick a day in my life - presumably the result of exceptionally hardy genes from either my alien grandmother or my extra-dimensional father. I had generally thought I was immune to communicable diseases but obviously I was mistaken. Something, maybe a pathogen inherent to this particular dimension, was clearly affecting me. I closed my eyes and rubbed my temples, trying to think.

"You look terrible," said a voice that was oddly familiar. I opened my eyes. My reflection in the mirror was staring at me, shaking his head in disapproval. "This is what comes of hanging out all night and not getting enough sleep."

"What?" I asked, stunned.

"You heard me," my reflection replied. "You had no business out there cavorting at the lake at all hours! It was past curfew anyway!"

"This can't be real," I said incredulously. This had to be a joke, some other prankster like Adam using an unknown ability to yank my chain. Or else I was going crazy.

"Oh no, it's real alright," the reflection said. "But it is a little crazy. Hmmm…I wonder how Electra feels about dating a guy who has conversations with his reflection."

Suddenly I was angry. "You leave her out of this!"

"And if I don't?"

Rather than reply, I screamed and flew at him, phasing in an attempt to imitate Alice and go through the looking glass and into the world of my reflection.

There were flashes of color and sound as I went through the mirror and my head swam for a few seconds. When the feeling passed, I was sitting on a park bench under the shade of a tree near a large pond. Dozens of ducks and geese swam on the water, honking and quacking loudly in a great cacophony of sound.

Something brushed against my ankle, swift and agile. I looked down, and saw that my foot was actually bare. In fact, I wasn't wearing anything except a pair of boxers. Something small, brown, and furry - a tiny rodent - twitched in the grass next to my foot.

"Mouse!" I shouted, making the small animal jump. Presumably this was what had brushed against me a second ago. It squeaked and then pressed up against my leg, trembling in fear. That's when I saw the snake.

It came slithering through the grass, heading towards the mouse. It was light blue in color, reminiscent of a swimming pool, with a single black eye on top of its head and one deadly silver fang centered in the roof of its mouth. I had never seen a serpent like it before. It slid through the grass with the fluidity of water, hissing evilly as it closed in on the mouse.

I reached for it with my hand, intending to grab it and toss it away. However, before I could get too close, it lunged. Its fang sank deep in my forearm, drawing blood. I screamed, both in pain and in anger, and teleported the snake away - where, I didn't know. The ducks and geese, having gone silent when I yelled, suddenly took off into mad flight in all directions, still honking and quacking loud enough to wake the dead.

My arm started throbbing almost immediately after the snake bit me. I stood up, not sure exactly where I was about to go, then collapsed to the ground. I drifted off into mindless, dreamless slumber.

Chapter 21

I woke up lying flat on my back on a cold, hard surface. I groaned and started to rise, realizing with a bit of a start that my back was actually bare.

It was pitch black, so I switched my vision over to infrared. One look around and I immediately knew where I was: the IV drip, the oxygen tank, and - most of all - the wheeled, adjustable hospital bed all let me know that I was in some type of infirmary. The cold, hard surface I had been sleeping on was actually a tiled floor.

I went over to the wall and turned the lights on, then switched my vision back to normal. At that point, I noticed that there was a dull, monotonous droning noise in the air. I quickly traced it to its source - a heart monitor. Although it was turned on, it wasn't connected to anything; that being the case, the machine was of the opinion that the patient had flatlined. Hence, the noise (which ceased when I turned the machine off).

I yawned, stretched, scratched my stomach. I was wearing a hospital gown, which someone had forgotten to tie up in the back. Thankfully, though, I still had my boxers on. I was absolutely famished, but other than that I felt a hundred times better than when I had last awakened. I rubbed my eyes and started walking towards a door that I believed was the entrance to the bathroom.

"Can you hear me in there?" said a disembodied voice unexpectedly. I looked around, surprised, but didn't immediately see the source. "Can you hear me?"

It was when the voice asked the question a second time that I noticed an intercom system on the wall next to the hospital bed.

The better to page you with, my dear...

I walked over and pressed the intercom button. "I can hear you." My voice sounded hoarse.

"Good, good," said the voice. "Listen, can you tell me where you are?"

"I'm in a hospital room," I said. "I don't know how I got here but...can you tell me what's going on?"

"Yes, but I need you to answer some questions first. Now, can you tell me your name?"

I thought about simply ignoring the voice - just teleporting out of there. But I didn't know what had happened, how I had gotten here. Also, I remembered feeling sick in my room, and I'd had perfect health up to that point. In short, I needed answers. I needed to play ball.

"Your name, please?" the voice asked again.

"Jim," I said. "Jim Carrow."

****

I spent approximately ten minutes answering basic questions - my age, where I go to school, who's the current president, and so on - until the person on the other end of the intercom achieved some level of comfort from my answers. Shortly thereafter, a medical team entered the room and I began to receive some of the answers I'd been wanting.

I was still at the Academy, and apparently I'd been in the school's infirmary for three days. I'd been brought in with an earth-scorching fever and completely delirious after someone found me wandering the school grounds in nothing but my boxers.

The docs had tried to get me set up in the hospital room where I'd woken up. However, after they attempted

155

to inject me with something to help the fever, I'd teleported the needle somewhere unknown and then telekinetically flung an orderly against the wall. Everyone had then fled the room, deeming me too dangerous to try to help at the moment. Someone had also turned off the lights when they left, presuming that I might hallucinate less if I couldn't see much of anything. (On the flip side, it was me turning on the lights that let the nurses on duty know I was conscious again.)

Now that I was lucid, the staff of the infirmary were able to safely fuss and fawn over me, and they did so. They took my temperature, tested reflexes, and so on before finally giving me a clean bill of health.

"You seem to be fine," said the doctor in charge, looking over my chart. He was young - probably late twenties, with "Manish Prasad, MD" on his name tag. "There were a few anomalies in your blood and physiology, but as best as we can tell, you are back to normal."

"Anomalies?" I muttered, eyes going wide. Outside of BT, almost no one had been privy to any type of medical diagnosis concerning me. I didn't need people knowing that I was part alien, because I had no intention of ending up spending the rest of my days as a government lab rat.

Dr. Prasad must have noted the look of concern on my face.

"Don't worry," he said. "Supers tend to have metabolisms and physiologies far different from normal people. A few anomalies are expected."

My relief was probably tangible, but I don't think he noticed.

"Your recovery, though, is good news in more ways than one," he said, continuing.

"How's that?"

"Well, we've had a number of other cases since you came in - none as severe as yours, you understand - but we can probably expect them to safely recover now. After you were brought in, we were on the lookout for an outbreak, so we probably caught it early in those other cases."

He was about to say something else when we both heard the rhythmic stomping of feet outside the room. Through the door, which was open, I saw four men go by in two-by-two formation, decked out in full riot gear.

"What's with the SWAT team?" I asked.

Dr. Prasad stepped over and closed the door before responding. "As I said, we didn't know what we were dealing with, and we really didn't have any infectious disease experts here, so we brought in help from the outside."

It took a second for the full ramifications to hit me. "You mean Earth? *Our* Earth? You brought a Gestapo unit over to help fight an illness?"

"No, we asked for help from the Centers for Disease Control. The team from the CDC - who will want to talk to you, by the way - brought the soldiers."

"Why? What do we need soldiers for?"

The doctor shrugged. "Crowd control, I guess. There was a chance that we'd have to quarantine people. We still might, so we've got a squad of soldiers setting up temporary barracks in the main courtyard."

I thought about that for a second, then remembered a question I'd had earlier. "I meant to ask, who brought me in?"

"A buddy of yours - a guy."

"My Campus Buddy? Adam Atom?"

The doctor suddenly looked like he had sat on a hot poker.

"What? Did I hurt Adam when he brought me in? Did I do something to him?"

The doctor seemed to be struggling to find his voice. He swallowed, then spoke.

"No, it wasn't Adam who brought you in. It was Smokescreen."

"But something's happened to Adam. What?"

The doctor swallowed again. "You've been out the past few days, so I guess there's no way you could have known…"

"What???!!" I screamed. It was all I could do not to grab him by the collar and shake him until he told me everything.

"Adam Atom's on lockdown, in a nullifier cell. He killed somebody."

MUTATION

Chapter 22

Going to see Adam totally freaked me out. Not because of what he had allegedly done, but because of where he was being held: a nullifier cell.

Nullifiers, as the name implies, nullify your powers. They take away your super abilities. I'd had to suffer through having my powers removed for a short time before, and calling it difficult would be an understatement. For supers, your powers are an element of your essence, as much as a part of you as an arm or a leg. In fact, losing your powers has often been described as like losing a limb.

Still, Adam was my friend, so I could take being in a nullifier cell - at least for a little while. In this instance, that meant going down to the basement, where the nullifier cells were. As I understood it, they were typically employed just to give students a timeout when they had been unruly or violated some mandate. They'd never been employed to hold a killer before.

Adam was sitting on a couch when they let me in to see him. As I said, the room was really meant to be the super equivalent of sending a bad student to the corner, so it wasn't as spartan as some nullifier cells I'd seen before. Aside from the couch, there were a couple of comfortable chairs, a desk, and some fully stocked bookshelves. A door set in a side wall presumably led to a bathroom.

I pulled up a chair and sat down in front of him. His eyes were puffy and red, an obvious indication that he had been crying. He looked at me, completely forlorn, and just broke down into tears.

"I just, I just don't know what happened," he said between sobs.

I placed a hand reassuringly on his shoulder. "Tell me."

Adam nodded, took a few seconds to compose himself, then blurted out the entire sad episode.

In short, he had decided to pull his infamous exploding pen stunt on another student. It was something he'd done a million times before so he wasn't concerned. The pen was supposed to gently burst and spill its contents on the anointed victim.

However, instead of a small pop, the pen had exploded like a stick of dynamite. The female student who was the subject of the prank was essentially blown apart, and four other people standing nearby were wounded. (For a second I harbored a fear that the victim had been Electra, but as Adam told his story, it became clear that it wasn't, and I sighed in obvious relief.) Adam, who had actually been close by when everything happened, had been as much in shock as anyone and had basically confessed on the spot.

All of this had occurred the previous day, while I had still been indisposed, and Adam had been in the nullifier ever since.

"Nothing like this has ever happened before," he said after telling his story. "I've always had *complete* control over my powers. But it's like my abilities were somehow amplified - ramped up."

"Have you tried using your powers since then?" I asked.

"No!" he practically screamed. "I've been too afraid to. Besides, I haven't left this room since it happened."

160

MUTATION

"There's got to be some explanation," I said.

"There is," he replied, voice full of regret. "I killed someone. Jim, what's going to happen to me?"

"I don't know," I said, shaking my head.

****

I left Adam a short time later and made my way to the cafeteria. I hadn't eaten in three days and was in desperate need of a meal. Still, I had consciously suppressed my hunger pangs in order to visit with Adam first.

Classes had been suspended because of the student who had been killed, but were set to resume the following day. That being the case, the hallways were full of people, and they were only discussing one thing: how Adam had killed a fellow student.

As it was late afternoon when I finally got there, the number of people in the cafeteria was quite small. After going through the service line, I found an unoccupied table and sat down to drown my sorrows in food. I went back through the line two more times and was considering doing so again when Electra stepped up and sat down beside me. I'd been so wrapped up in my own thoughts that I hadn't even noticed her come in.

She didn't say anything, just leaned over and gave me a hug that I returned. Then we just sat there quietly for a few moments, with her holding my hand.

"Hey," she finally said, touching my face. "Penny for your thoughts."

I sighed despondently. "This is all so crazy! Nothing makes sense! First, I get sick and end up hospitalized? I *never* get sick! And now Adam..."

"That's not your fault. None of it's your fault. You didn't choose to get sick. You didn't make Adam do what he did. It's just the way of the world. Things happen."

She was right, of course, but I didn't feel like I should just accept it. I wanted to do something. Instead, I just sat there and let Electra silently console me.

After a while, I caught her glancing at her watch.

"I know you probably have things to do," I said. "Don't feel obligated to sit here and hold my hand. Literally."

She smiled. "Thanks. Have dinner with me later?"

I nodded and watched as she walked out. Then I teleported myself to my room. I stretched out on the bed, only intending to rest my eyes for a minute, but before I knew it, I was asleep.

MUTATION

Chapter 23

I awoke to the sound of a deep, reverberating rumbling. I lay still for a moment, trying to ascertain whether it was something real or the remnant of a dream. The sound came again. *Definitely real.* Moreover, I recognized it for what it was: an explosion.

I jumped up and shifted into super speed, then zoomed from the room, heading straight to the main lobby of the school. Once there, I decelerated back to normal speed, trying to get a fix on where the explosions had come from. If I were in a place filled with normal people, I'd be able to pinpoint the source of the problem by noting the direction that people were running *from*. Here, students were running every which way, as some apparently tried to flee the danger and others were willing to face it. A bevy of screams coming from the cafeteria area caught my attention. I teleported there.

An odd scene greeted me when I popped in. Adam was in the center of the room, leaning on a table for support. He was covered in sweat, and seemed to be straining to hold himself upright. Groups of students were frightfully clustered against the walls all around the room, trying to stay as far away from him as possible. Some of the cooking staff were peeking out of the windows in the two swinging doors that led to the kitchen.

As I watched, the table Adam was leaning on began to splinter and come violently apart in little bursts as a sound like firecrackers going off rippled across its surface. Finally it exploded, sending splinters and wood chips flying everywhere, and eliciting another round of screams from a group of girls near the window.

Empathically, I felt anxiety pouring off him, as well as anguish and - surprisingly - steely determination. But most of all I felt fear. I ran towards him.

"Keep away from him!" somebody yelled, but I ignored them.

Despite the shouted warning, Adam didn't seem to notice me until I was practically in front of him. Relief, sudden and unexpected, flooded out of him and hit me in a deluge of emotion as he practically collapsed against me.

"Please…" he muttered, his entire body tense with strain. "Please…"

He didn't seem to be able to say more, so I peeked inside his mind, not daring to go too far because of my own limitations. My eyes went wide and I stared at him.

"Get back!" I shouted at the crowd of onlookers. Then I wrapped Adam in my power and teleported both of us to the lake where we'd all hung out just a few days before. I telescoped my vision as far as I could and, looking in the direction opposite the school, picked a point on the horizon - a small, grassy hill - and teleported us there. With my vision still telescoped, I looked to the horizon and once again teleported us to the farthest place I could see - this time a large, open field.

The tension left Adam as if swept out with a broom and he collapsed to his knees.

"Thank…thank you," he said. I knelt next to him and put and arm around his shoulder. Then I turned my head, closed my eyes and phased, becoming insubstantial as a small popping noise began coming from where Adam was kneeling.

****

MUTATION

I later learned that the explosion - despite how far I'd teleported us - had still been heard and felt at the Academy. Afterwards, I just stayed there for a long time - floating at the center of the giant, smoking crater Adam's death had created - crying. I stayed there crying until the ringing in my ears died down. I stayed there crying until the blackened, scorched earth started to cool. I stayed there crying until my eyes fully recovered from the brilliant white flash that had accompanied Adam's passing and penetrated even my closed eyelids.

All in all, I stayed the night and a good part of the next day there. Finally, when it seemed that I was all out of tears, I decided I needed to go back.

Hungry after my ordeal, I teleported to the cafeteria. It was officially well past lunchtime, but there were usually a number of late stragglers still dining. This time, the place was empty. Not just devoid of students, but *completely* deserted. When I stepped through the swinging doors that led to the kitchen, there weren't even any staff in the usual process of preparing dinner.

Although surprised not to see anyone, I was still determined to get something to eat. After a few seconds of wandering, I saw a large door that seemed to lead to a walk-in refrigerator. Inside, I found a bunch of vegetables, fruit, uncooked meat and so on. I went back out into the kitchen and pulled a large mixing bowl down from a cooking rack. I took it into the walk-in and filled it with grapes, apples, and bananas.

I left the kitchen with my bowl of loot, eating as I walked. Now that I took a good look around, I noticed that the place was kind of a mess. Tables and chairs were overturned, presumably the result of students trying to distance themselves from Adam. Half-eaten morsels of food and spilled drinks littered the floor. And splintered wood was everywhere.

I walked next door to the student break room. Like the cafeteria, it was empty. Now I was starting to get worried. Something was definitely wrong. I quickly wolfed down the rest of the food in my bowl, then decided to visit the admin office. I was tempted to teleport there, but decided to walk on the off-chance that I'd bump into someone who could tell me what was going on.

Decision made, I stepped out of the break room and almost ran into a couple of the SWAT guys.

"Freeze!" they both yelled in stereo, as well as bringing up their semi-assault rifles. I almost gave in to a knee-jerk reaction to teleport away. However, I was trying to find out what was going on, so instead I slowly raised my hands, careful not to make any threatening gestures.

"What are you doing here?" one of them asked.

"I'm a student," I said.

"No, why aren't you complying with the quarantine?"

Quarantine?

The look on my face must have made it clear that I didn't know what he was talking about.

"What's your name, kid?" he asked.

"Jim. Jim Carrow."

I saw a strange look pass between the two of them.

"You need to come with us."

Chapter 24

The SWAT guys escorted me to Magnavolt's conference room. I was told to wait inside while they took up positions outside the door. A moment later, Magnavolt practically flew into the room.

"Jim!" he exclaimed, clapping me on the shoulder. "You're alright!"

"Yeah, I'm fine," I said, somewhat perplexed by his excitement.

"They told me you teleported away with Adam. Afterwards, there was the explosion, and when you didn't come back…"

Now I understood his initial giddiness. He'd thought I was dead. We both took a seat at the conference table.

"Adam…?" he asked. I simply shook my head. It wasn't something I wanted to talk about just yet.

Regardless, before anything more could be said, Dr. Prasad entered the room, accompanied by a middle-aged man with thinning, iron-gray hair. The man wore a lab coat and had a hard look about him. Something about him seemed familiar, but I couldn't put my finger on it.

"Is this him?" the man asked, without waiting for introductions.

"Yes," replied Dr. Prasad.

"Then let's get him to the lab," the man said. "As soon as he's there–"

"Hold up," I interjected. I really didn't like them talking about me like I wasn't in the room. "What exactly is going on here?"

The man in the lab coat looked at me as if seeing me for the first time. I felt a certain arrogance and

167

cockiness drifting out from him, as if he only deigned to speak with his peers or better. I immediately got a bad feeling about him.

Before the silence got awkward, Magnavolt spoke up. "Jim, I think you already know Dr. Prasad." I nodded at the good doctor. "This other gentleman is Dr. Aldiss. He's one of the world's foremost virologists and an expert on infectious diseases. He's here to help us with this bug that seems to be going around."

"It's more than just some bug," Aldiss chimed in. "It's a highly contagious organism that – at the moment – is posing a threat to almost everyone here. That's why I declared a quarantine."

"*You* declared a quarantine?" I asked, then looked at Magnavolt quizzically.

"I've handed over all authority of the Academy – all facilities, all resources, all personnel – to Dr. Aldiss and his team," Magnavolt said in response to the expression on my face. "They're running the show."

I shook my head in disbelief. We had just thumbed our nose at a government organization a week earlier during our little conference with Pace. Why would we now invite another government agency to come in and take over?

"You have to understand, Jim," Prasad interposed. "We're in over our heads on this thing. This virus, it seems to attack the metagene in supers – the gene that's the origin of their powers. It's mutating the gene, making their powers unstable. One of our students, Glacia, almost froze three of her classmates to death. Another kid almost asphyxiated everyone in the cafeteria when he sucked all the air out of the room."

"So you just hand this guy the reins? That was the best solution?" I asked. I hadn't meant it rhetorically, but no one responded. Aldiss suddenly looked like he wanted to say something, but I didn't give him a chance. "What about the Alpha League and the other superhero teams? What do they say about this?"

Magnavolt sighed. "They don't know. We can't reach them."

I was stunned. "What do you mean you can't reach them?"

Magnavolt sighed. "Yesterday, as you already know, Adam somehow got out of the nullifier room he was in. With his powers back, he – for some strange reason – decided to blow up the transdimensional gateway, the vortex phones, and the communication interface."

"So that means…" I trailed off as the full ramifications of what he was saying hit me.

"Yes," he continued. "We can't communicate with Earth. Even worse, we're stuck here."

Chapter 25

I couldn't believe what I was hearing, and it clearly showed on my face.

"It's not that bad, Jim," Magnavolt said, attempting to sound reassuring. "Given time, we can repair the vortex gate. It's the virus that's the pressing issue at the moment."

"And that's where you come in," said Aldiss, seemingly happy that he was now getting a chance to speak. "We've had a few issues with students losing control, but – based on your personal experience with it - we basically think that the virus has a short life cycle."

"How short?" I asked.

"Roughly three days," he said, "give or take. But that's primarily based on what happened to you, since you were the first infected."

"So what, you're labeling me as patient zero in this thing?"

Aldiss suddenly looked stern. "It obviously began somewhere. Right now, you appear to be the origin, so we need to get you to our lab, run some blood work–"

"Not gonna happen," I said, shaking my head and crossing my arms defiantly. I had a singularly unique physiology, from the cellular level on up. If anybody like Aldiss ever got me into a lab, I was never going to get out if they could help it. "I'm willing to help, but I'm not about to be poked and prodded like some human guinea pig."

Aldiss put his hands on the conference table and leaned forward with something akin to maniacal glee in his eyes.

"You don't have a choice," he said.

"Wanna bet?" I replied.

Aldiss straightened up. "Guards," he yelled over his shoulder in the direction of the doorway. The two guys who had escorted me to the conference room appeared. "Take this student up to the lab we've set up in the infirmary. If he tries anything, shoot him – but try to make it a flesh wound, since we prefer to have him alive."

I snorted contemptuously – obviously Aldiss didn't know who I was – then teleported back to my room.

MUTATION

Chapter 26

My initial thought after I teleported was that I'd made a mistake. I had intended to pop back to my own room, but I'd obviously done something wrong and ended up in someone else's, because – while I was definitely in a dorm room – I found myself in the midst of some students who I wasn't acquainted with.

There were four of them. The first was about my height, but with a bald head and Asian features. He was standing near the window and wearing a long-sleeved, black Mandarin shirt with white cuffs and matching pants.

There was also a willowy blonde with elfin ears (like my mother), sitting at the desk. She wore a form-fitting two-piece outfit that left her arms bare from the shoulders down. I also couldn't help but notice that she carried what appeared to be two ornamental daggers, one sheathed at either hip.

The last two were guys, and they were seated next to each other on the bed. One had on a golf shirt and cargo pants and was chewing gum. The other seemed familiar to me, and then I recognized him: it was the kid who had brought us the drinks at the lake party a few nights back.

I took in all of this in the space of a few seconds, then found myself occupied by the thought that this might be the virus at work. Had I lost control of my powers? Was I unable to teleport where I intended anymore? But then I noticed small nuances that set my mind at ease: the angle of the blinds on the window; the sheets on the bed; most of all, the box of candy bars on the dresser. This was indeed my room. I wasn't the interloper; they were.

They all seemed to notice me simultaneously. The girl at my desk was on her feet immediately, blades drawn and glowing. Next to her stood the guy in the cargo pants, holding his hands in front of him at chest level, left over right, with a glowing sphere between them. The other two stood behind them. Reacting to their aggressiveness, I got ready to shift into super speed.

"Stop," said the guy in the Mandarin shirt. He didn't shout or speak forcefully, but his voice resonated. He stepped out from behind his companions. "There is no need for conflict."

The girl with the daggers and the boy in the cargo pants exchanged glances, then slowly came out of their fighting stances. Her daggers stopped glowing as she put them away, and the sphere of light between the guy's hands - and I now saw that he had an odd assortment of rings on his fingers - dissipated.

A million questions bubbled up in my brain, but before I could ask a single one of them, the guy in the Mandarin shirt spoke.

"You would like an explanation for our presence here," he said, "and we will gladly give it. But it is not safe to speak here. Will you trust us enough to come with us?"

Oddly enough, I couldn't read him empathically; he gave off absolutely no emotion. That was rare and unusual, but not completely unknown to me. Just as there is training that builds shields around your mind so that you don't broadcast your thoughts, one can also learn to harness emotions and keep them in check. Still, there was a certain sincerity in his voice that made me feel he was

173

trustworthy. Moreover, I got an odd sensation that what they had to tell me was important.

"I'll come," I said after a moment.

The guy in the Mandarin shirt nodded at the girl. She drew one of her daggers, closed her eyes, and began muttering in a language I didn't understand. The dagger began to glow red. Without warning, she shouted and then swung the blade in arc through the air in front of her, as if striking at something that only she could see.

Amazingly, the air itself seemed to part in a jagged red line that ran vertically for about five feet before ending about six inches above the floor. The girl gave a smug grin to the guy in the cargo pants, who stuck out his tongue at her. Then she stepped into the opening she had created and disappeared.

The kid from the lake party went through next, followed by the fellow in the cargo pants. The guy in the Mandarin shirt bowed his head slightly and made a you-first gesture with his hand. I took a deep breath and stepped through.

****

We came out in a good-sized, well-lit but windowless room. There was a workstation in one corner which housed a computer and related equipment. A sofa and a couple of lounge chairs were arranged around a coffee table near one of the walls. A miniature fridge was plugged in near a small desk that was covered with books and papers. Two side doors - set facing each other - apparently led to additional rooms. There was a stack of chairs pushed against one of the other walls, along with some filing cabinets and other miscellaneous items. In the center of the room were several cafeteria tables pushed together, with a couple of laptop computers on top and a half-dozen chairs around them. I would later learn that the room was a sub-basement storage unit (which explained the lack of windows) that my new friends had converted for their own use.

Unlike teleportation, which was instantaneous, the trip here had seemed to take a few seconds. During that time, I experienced a slight feeling of disorientation, as I just seemed to be traveling through a bleak zone of emptiness where I was robbed of all senses – sight, sound, etc. And then we'd come out.

Almost immediately, the guy in the cargo pants and the elfin girl began arguing about some aspect of the journey we had just taken. The other two ignored them, and the one in the Mandarin shirt turned to me.

"Thank you for trusting us," he said. "Now that we are here, we can be formally introduced. My name is Li. The young man and woman arguing are Kane and Gossamer, respectively. The other young man is Gavin."

Gavin, now seated at the workstation, waved. "Sorry, I don't have a cool superhero name yet."

"I'm Jim," I said. "Can you tell me now what you were doing in my room?"

"Waiting for you, of course," said Li.

"But why?"

"Because we require your help to save the school – or rather, everyone in it."

Chapter 27

I was a little surprised at Li's statement, but managed to recover rather quickly.

"Assuming you're talking about the virus, that's a little over-dramatic, don't you think?"

"No, it's an understatement, if anything," Gossamer replied.

"Come on," I said. "There have definitely been some incidents, but that CDC guy, Dr. Aldiss, says that this thing should run its course in a few days."

"Yeah, ask Adam Atom how that worked out," said Kane. I felt my blood start to boil at the mention of Adam, while Gossamer smacked Kane on the arm and gave a vigorous nod in my direction. Kane frowned for a second, and then his mouth dropped open as he realized I was the guy who had teleported Adam away. "I'm sorry…"

"Don't worry about it," I said, trying to keep all emotion out of my voice. "Just bring me up to speed."

"Very well," Li stated flatly. "I am aware of the prognosis of Dr. Aldiss, but I firmly believe him to be mistaken. The virus in question attaches to the metagene in supers and mutates it in such a way that it can affect their powers."

"Affects them how?" I asked. Prasad had said something similar, but I'd been too angry at the time to focus or ask questions about it.

"Thus far, it can either decrease their abilities substantially or increase them by an order of magnitude. But, over time, as the virus mutates the metagene, their abilities will become more unstable. They will eventually lose control of them altogether."

I suddenly had a very good idea of what had happened to Adam.

Li went on. "Even more, their entire DNA structure will start unraveling."

"Unraveling?" I asked. "What does that mean?"

"It means they'll die," said Gossamer.

****

Over the next fifteen minutes, Li and his friends gave me a very thorough education regarding the virus. In addition to either increasing or decreasing a super's powers, there was a third class of infected people within whom the virus still attached to the metagene but appeared to be dormant. Moreover, the five of us were the only uninfected students in the entire school. (Although technically, I had been infected but had recovered.)

"How do you guys know all this?" I finally asked Li when we stopped to take a break. Gossamer and Kane were over by the mini-fridge, arguing. Gavin was at the computer workstation.

"I hacked the mainframe of the infirmary. It contained all of the accumulated information that the medical staff had gathered on the virus."

"Why'd you do that - bored?"

"In actuality, I thought I could be of assistance, so I proffered my services in the wake of the freezing incident involving Glacia. However, my offer to serve as a volunteer was rebuffed."

"So you hacked your way in. Well, I'll say one thing for you, you're persistent. But what makes you so sure that you're right and Aldiss is wrong about the hazard posed by the virus?"

"With the data I collected, I ran exactly one thousand, three hundred seventy-seven simulations. In each instance, the virus eventually spread to the entire student body and killed them all."

"Obviously not everybody, since you guys are immune."

"I should elaborate. After I ran my simulations, Aldiss had the entire school tested. I hacked back in to find out the extent of the infection and whether my simulations were accurate. That is when I found the records of the others here indicating that they were uninfected."

"So it was you who assembled this little ragtag army."

"Correct."

"Well, if you really needed someone to help, why not get some of the big guns, like Dynamo?"

"Would Adam Atom have been a good choice for our 'army'?"

I frowned, clenching my fist. Then understanding dawned on me. "Of course not. Adam would have been a poor choice because his powers were unstable due to the virus. He blew himself up, even though his powers weren't supposed to have an effect on the atoms of living things."

"Yes. Any infected person might be just as likely to harm us – whether intentionally or not – as to help us. They would be a liability."

"Still, I should go visit my friends - Electra and Smokey - and let them know what's going on."

"I would advise against that."

178

I raised an eyebrow. "Don't you think they deserve to know?"

Rather than answer the question, Li asked one of his own. "Have you ever known someone to have such a strong emotional reaction to something that it affected them physically?"

"Yeah," I said, after thinking for a moment. "In fifth grade, Molly Lewis became so nervous about a speech she had to give that she threw up."

"So you would agree that emotions can affect you physically?"

"Of course."

"And for a super, can strong emotions affect the use and control of their powers?"

"Yes," I agreed, reflecting back on the day I took Electra to Paris and she twice became so excited that the air became charged. I sighed. "I see your point. Telling my friends about the virus might balloon their emotions in some way and destabilize their metagene."

"I'm glad you understand."

"But I should at least go see them - let them know I'm okay."

"Okay?" he repeated.

"Yeah. Magnavolt said he thought I'd been killed when I didn't come back, so they're probably thinking the same thing."

"And when they see that you are not dead, do you think they will be excited?"

"Probably, if they thought I was…" My voice trailed off as I saw what he was getting at. Seeing me alive might get them excited, and excitement might affect the stability of the metagene.

"You are right to be concerned," Li said, "but it is best that you avoid your friends for now. We can best help them by being successful in what we are now contemplating."

"I still don't know what this plan of yours is," I said.

Li was about to say something when Kane and Gossamer approached us.

"The fridge is almost empty, so we're going on a food run," Kane said. "Anyone want anything in particular?" Both Li and I shook our heads in the negative, while Gavin said something about fresh fruit. Kane and Gossamer, in heated debate about something, headed towards a door that had an "Exit" sign above it.

"What's their story?" I asked as Kane and Gossamer left.

"Ostensibly, they are bitter adversaries with respect to whether the human sorcery employed by Kane rivals the elfin magic wielded by Gossamer. In actuality, they are romantically attracted to each other and unsure of how to express it."

"So instead they argue all the time. It's the teen version of little kids who hit the person they like."

"That is an accurate analogy."

"What about him?" I nodded towards Gavin, who seemed to be staring at the computer at the workstation. In my opinion, Gavin was a bit of an odd duck. I had noticed when we were at the table talking about the virus that he acted as if he were afraid to come near me.

"Gavin has an inherent ability to interact with computers, even without an interface such as a keyboard. Thus, I believe he spends an inordinate amount of time online playing games and such. The result, however, is that he has developed into being what you might term 'socially awkward.' He has yet to learn how to comfortably interact or engage with others."

I smiled to myself, reflecting on the fact that just a few minutes earlier I had thought something similar about Li because his manner of speech seemed stilted and gauche. Then I'd realized what it was that seemed off to me: Li spoke almost entirely without contractions.

"Back to the plan," I said, changing the subject. "I still don't know exactly what it is you're trying to do."

"Before I recruited the others, I tried to present my findings to the medical staff at the infirmary."

"Let me guess. They didn't take you seriously."

"That is a correct assumption."

"Well, why should they? Why should I, for that matter? What makes you more qualified than a world-class virologist?"

"I have PhD-level expertise in twenty-three fields, including medicine, chemistry, physics, bio-mechanics—"

"Alright, alright, alright. Let's say I believe you. Now what?"

"Like myself, I assume Dr. Aldiss and his team have run simulations concerning the virus. Compared to the modeling software they are using, my own constructs are rather crude and primitive, but I do not possess the time or the resources to significantly improve them. However, I think that if I can use their own modeling software to obtain the same results as my simulations, then the CDC team will be more inclined to listen."

"So you want to steal a computer program."

"More or less."

I shrugged. "I guess you can count me in. And no offense, but I hope you're wrong."

"So do I."

"Well, if you are right about how deadly this thing is, at least the outbreak happened here – at the Academy – where we're sealed off."

"Yes," Li said. "That is rather convenient."

Something about his tone caught my attention. "What are you trying to say?"

"There are a number of coincidences here that go beyond the expected levels of probability in terms of random occurrence."

I frowned, thinking about what Li had just said. "Are you trying to say that this is deliberate? That someone is doing this?"

Li inclined his head thoughtfully. "We have an isolated environment, a genetically unique population for the most part, and a pathogen that only affects *that* population."

Li was dropping hints, trying to get me to figure it out on my own. When I did, the answer hit me like a freight train.

"A lab experiment," I mumbled. "The whole school is a lab experiment."

"That is my conclusion," Li said. "With at least three different experimentation groups: those with a dormant version of the virus, those with increased powers, and those with decreased powers."

It all made sense, and yet…it felt like we were missing something. I thought back to my science classes over the years, trying to remember how experiments were conducted, and then it came to me.

"If this is just one big experiment like you said, then where's the control?"

"The control? You mean the control *group*? The one that doesn't get infected in an experiment like this?"

"Yes. Where are they?"

Li seemed to ponder this momentarily, then pulled over one of the laptops on the table and began typing. After a few moments, he turned it towards me. The screen was covered with a long list of names

"I'm pulling this from the information I hacked. Previously, I screened the data only for individuals who had been exposed but were uninfected and therefore immune. The list before you is a list of people who have *not* been exposed at all."

"The control group," I said. I looked at the list, unsure of who many of these people were. Then I came across names I recognized - like Magnavolt - and understood. It was the faculty and staff.

Chapter 28

The modeling software Li wanted was apparently kept on an isolated computer system that the CDC team had brought over with them. It was not connected to the infirmary's mainframe, so he hadn't been able to hack in and retrieve it. Basically, someone had to physically go in and get it.

After Gossamer and Kane had returned with some food (presumably from the cafeteria), we'd had a short meal before resuming with our plans. Now the rest of us stood huddled around Li, who sat at the computer workstation.

"There," Li said, pointing to the screen. "That is the area we need to get into."

He had just hacked into the infirmary's system again – this time the live video feed from various cameras. What he was indicating was an obviously-locked door that was also manned by two armed guards.

"It is essentially a dual security system," Li went on. "There is a scanner on each side of the door, and both have to give a green light before the door will unlock. In addition, each guard is authorized to visually observe the scan to ensure that no one is trying to bypass the protocol."

I was surprised at what I was seeing. "Dual security, cameras…since when do we need all that in the medical wing?"

"They were not in place before," said Li. "However, the wing was already pre-wired for them, as is much of the school. All Aldiss had to do was install the necessary equipment and activate it."

Li went back to typing, and the scene on the screen changed. We were now looking at a room with large glass walls that allowed us to see clearly inside. Against the far wall of the room was a large bank of computers. The rest of the interior contained a lab table and a few workstations.

"I take it that's the room we have to get in," said Kane. Li nodded.

"Well, if that's the room, why don't we just let Jim here teleport in and get what we need?" asked Gavin. It was one of the few occasions on which I'd heard him speak since joining their little group. However, he clearly wasn't comfortable with me yet, as he seemed to be trying to keep as much distance between himself and me as possible.

"For starters," I said, "I haven't been in that area before. I've never laid actual eyeballs on it."

"Yes, but I've heard you can teleport to places you haven't been based on an image," Gavin said.

"True, I've done it before," I admitted. "But I basically walked into a trap." I spent a brief moment reflecting on the one time I'd done what Gavin was suggesting, and had teleported myself into a nullifier cell. As far as I was concerned, that option was off the table.

"Teleporting in is probably not a viable plan," Li said. "We have to assume someone is watching via the cameras at all times. For that same reason, the magic Gossamer utilizes to occasionally move from place to place would not be helpful. Moreover, Dr. Aldiss is generally the only person who goes in this room, so the presence of anyone else in there would raise suspicion."

"So, if we can't go in the room, how do we get the program?" Gossamer asked.

"With this," Li responded, producing a small, black box made of hardened plastic with a glowing red LED on it. "If we can get this device within twenty feet of the room's main computer bank, it will automatically download the modeling software."

"In other words, we don't need to go in the room," Kane observed.

"Exactly," Li replied. "But the device has to stay in range until the LED turns green, or the entire download will be aborted."

****

Since we needed two people to get past the dual-security checkpoint, I initially volunteered, thinking that my shapeshifting ability would be useful. Li told me that it wouldn't help.

"I am aware that you can duplicate the appearance of someone else," he said, "but can you replicate them down to the cellular level?"

"What do you mean?"

"Apparently you weren't paying close enough attention," Gossamer said. "That checkpoint is a retinal scanner. Unless you can duplicate someone's retinal print, shapeshifting won't help us here."

Actually I *could* duplicate a retinal pattern - if I had a model to work off of, like a close-up, detailed photo. But since we didn't have anything like that it didn't seem to be worth mentioning.

"Then how do we get past the checkpoint?" I asked.

"Magic," Kane said with a smile and a flourish of his arm that made Gossamer roll her eyes.

It turned out that the plan was to have Kane cast a glamour over two of us. Using hair from two members of the CDC staff, his magic would not only replicate the appearance of the CDC personnel in question, but also their genetic structure.

"How'd you get hair from these people?" I asked.

"My magic gave us access to the rooms," Gossamer replied. I nodded, remembering how we'd traveled from my room to our current digs.

"That's about the only thing that elfin mumbo jumbo is good for," Kane snidely remarked.

Gossamer ignored him. "Once inside, we simply raided their combs and brushes. Shortly after that, we went to your room to wait for you."

Silently, I applauded their efforts, impressed by what they had accomplished. While I was wrapped in my own thoughts, the others began discussing who should go on the mission with me. Ultimately, they drew straws, with Gossamer getting the shortest.

Thereafter, it was a bit of a waiting game. The guards currently on duty at the dual checkpoint would have an idea of who was already inside, so we couldn't put our plan into action until there was a shift change.

According to Li, the changing of the guard took place every four hours. About five minutes before it was to occur, Kane worked his magic on us.

First, he retrieved several plastic bags from one of the filing cabinets in the room. I could see that they all seemed to contain hair. Kane then pulled a few strands from one of the bags with his right hand and then repeated the process with another bag using his left hand. He closed his eyes and began chanting rhythmically in an unknown tongue, holding his clenched palms in front of him.

As his voice continued its sing-song melody, his hands began to glow with a soft, azure light and the air around him seemed to vibrate.

Continuing to chant, he opened his eyes and stepped forward, placing the hairs in his right hand on my head. Then he did the same to Gossamer with the hairs in his left.

There was an odd numbing sensation that started at my head and spread its way down. At the same time, a small cascade of warm sparks seemed to fall about me, like a glittery flurry of snowflakes that vanished when they hit the floor. I looked myself over, but couldn't see any change.

"It didn't work," I said. Gavin and Kane looked at me and laughed. So did Gossamer – or at least, I thought it was Gossamer. Where the elf had stood a moment before there was now a demure redhead in a white lab coat. Obviously the spell had worked on her but not me. But what was so funny?

"It worked," said Li, the only one of my colleagues who didn't have a grin on his face. "Your self-image – the way you see yourself – may not have changed, but to everyone else you are now a portly research assistant with an unevenly-shaven goatee."

"And how do I look?" asked Gossamer.

Kane said something that I didn't quite catch, but which made Gossamer give him an evil look while Gavin burst out laughing. As Gossamer began to reply, Li pulled me aside.

"I would like to ask that you take particular care in looking out for Gossamer on this mission," he said.

I was a little surprised. Thus far I had garnered the impression that Gossamer was some kind of elfin warrior and that she could take care of herself. I said as much to Li.

"I have no reason to disagree with you for the most part," he said, "but do you recall our discussion regarding someone using the Academy and the student population as a lab?"

"Yes, of course," I replied.

"Then you must recognize that immune test subjects are quite likely beyond anything they expected to encounter."

"So what are you thinking? That whoever's behind this will try to capture her?"

"Capture…or eliminate her. Everyone in this room, in fact. It's part of the reason we've been hiding out down here."

"But how would they even know anyone's immune?"

"If it is an experiment, it would be an exercise in futility for those in charge if they could not glean any information from it. Presumably then, they have access to the data – perhaps from hacking, as I did."

"Do you think they may also have access to the cameras?"

"I'm torn between saying 'possibly' and 'probably.' I will venture to say probably."

"I guess that's just an extra incentive to get this done fast."

MUTATION

Chapter 29

As plans go, this one started off about as well as you could hope for. I teleported Gossamer and myself to one of the seldom-used stairwells, and then we walked over to the infirmary. Along the way, we passed several two-man patrol units, but no one ever stopped us, so apparently we looked the part.

Once at the infirmary, we breezed past the initial checkpoint. I had to admit that I was a little nervous during the retinal scan and ready to teleport us out of there, but we got a green light and entered the secure section.

Once inside, we hit our first speed bump. We were in a bit of an open foyer, with hallways branching off in three directions.

I groaned audibly. Despite all our planning, we had failed to look at a single, solitary map, floor plan, or blueprint. I guess we'd been under the assumption that we would walk in and see the right room immediately. No such luck!

"Let's go," I muttered softly, and we began walking down one of the hallways.

It took ten minutes of random walking, but we finally located the right room. It was actually one of a suite of similarly designed rooms off the center hallway we had observed earlier. Fortunately, we'd had little trouble en route to finding it. On a couple of occasions, someone had waved at us saying, "Hey, Chris," or "Hi, Terry," but no one tried to engage us in conversation. (Which would have been bad, since we didn't know who was who. What were the odds of being glamoured into a man and woman who both had androgynous names?)

Outside the room, I pulled out the download device. It wasn't making any noise, but the red LED light was flashing and it was vibrating softly. Inside the room, I didn't notice much different than what we'd seen on camera, except now there was an open laptop on the lab table.

I looked around and located the camera we had used to view the room earlier. I was tempted to get in its line of sight and wave, but quickly remembered that our group wasn't the only one using the cameras. The thought made me nervous in more ways than one, and when I casually surveyed the area we were in I saw other cameras in place.

"Stay here," I whispered to Gossamer, handing her Li's downloader. I stepped into one of the nearby rooms and looked around. On a table I saw a clipboard with some type of printout attached. It was just what we needed. I grabbed it and headed back towards Gossamer.

"As I was saying," I uttered in what I hoped was a natural-sounding voice and tapping the clipboard for emphasis, "these electrolytes are way too high—"

"What are you doing??!!" Gossamer hissed, cutting me off.

"Trying to act natural," I replied in a hushed tone. "Us standing here next to each other, not doing anything and not talking, is far from natural. And our public is watching."

Gossamer followed my glance to one of the other cameras. Her demeanor changed almost instantaneously.

"Please, go on," she said, looking at me in rapt attention.

I went back to uttering complete nonsense while waiting for the downloader to do its thing. Unfortunately,

Li hadn't been able to give an estimate of how long it would take; it had to find the right software first and then the download would begin. However, he'd said it shouldn't take longer than fifteen minutes.

Personally, I felt that a quarter of an hour was a long time to stand in front of cameras doing next to nothing, and the clipboard act would only work for so long. Still, I thought there was a chance that we could pull it off. That's when the whole thing came apart.

The first indication that things might not necessarily end neatly came about three minutes after we'd been in place, when we heard footsteps coming down the hall. Heavy, booted footsteps. Even more, I picked up on a set of strong emotions tied to a demeanor and attitude that I recognized. At that moment, Estrella came through the doorway that led to the suite of rooms we were in, followed by a quartet of armed guards who held their weapons at the ready. They clearly had not come to talk.

On my part, I was almost frozen in shock at seeing Estrella here at the Academy. Gossamer, on the other hand, exploded into action. In one fluid motion, she tossed me the downloader and drew her daggers, which were glowing with an eerie, eldritch light. Her elfin magic was obviously incompatible with Kane's sorcery, because the glamour dissolved around her like butter melting in a hot skillet. A spark of blue light shot from one of her daggers, striking one of the guards and blowing him back out through the doorway.

Estrella fired a laser beam at her, which Gossamer deflected with one of her blades. It went right back at Estrella, striking her in the face. Estrella let out an ear-splitting scream of agony that brought me back to myself, putting her hands up to her eyes at the same time. A second later she vanished, obviously teleporting herself to safety.

I wrapped Gossamer in my power, preparing to teleport us out of there when a gentle vibration in my hand reminded me of the downloader. I couldn't leave until it finished getting the modeling software. In fact, I really couldn't move very far without going beyond its twenty-foot limit.

By now the guards had started firing, bullets shattering the glass that made up the walls of most of the rooms. Instinctively, I ducked down. Still on her feet, Gossamer had her head down, holding her daggers crossed in front of her. A transparent shield had formed around her, deflecting all the bullets that would otherwise have ripped her to shreds. Unfortunately, it looked like her shield was about to fade.

I set the downloader on the floor and shifted into super speed. I stood up, then zipped over to Gossamer, sidestepping bullets along the way. I teleported the remaining three guards to the lake (actually dumping them *in* the lake), then shifted back down to normal speed, making Gossamer and myself insubstantial at the same time. A few bullets whizzed harmlessly through us, and then there was silence.

Gossamer looked confused for a moment, but apparently accepted the fact that all of our adversaries were out of commission at the moment.

"Come on," I said, as we went back to where I'd set the downloader on the floor, broken glass crackling under our feet.

The downloader was gone.

I glanced around, and then I saw it. Or rather, the remains of it.

The plastic casing had shattered into a dozen tiny pieces. Broken wires stuck out like wild blades of grass in an open field.

It was obvious what had happened. One of the bullets had ricocheted and hit the downloader, effectively destroying it.

"Now what?" asked Gossamer, as I sat there holding the pieces of the device in my hand. Before I could respond, a trio of guards came into the suite, firing.

We ducked into the room containing the computers with the modeling software. The machines themselves didn't seem to have been touched by the random gunfire. Moreover, the laptop I'd seen earlier was still sitting on the lab table. Taken with a sudden inspiration, I grabbed the laptop and tucked it under my arm. Then I teleported us back to the sub-basement room.

When we arrived, I didn't have to explain what had happened to the download device; they had seen on the camera. I handed Li the laptop, while Kane checked on Gossamer.

"What is this?" Li asked.

"I don't know, but it was in that room," I said. "I remember you saying that Aldiss was the only one who ever really went in there, so I figured it might be important."

I suddenly felt exhausted; I couldn't remember the last time I'd slept. I'd been told that one of the side rooms contained some sleeping cots, so I announced that I was going to take a nap. Before I could get to the proper door, however, Kane came over and grabbed me by the arm, almost in anger.

"Why didn't you teleport Gossamer out of there?" he asked, trying to keep his voice low.

"What are you talking about?" I asked, shaking off his grip.

"When the bullets started flying, why didn't you teleport her out of there?"

"I had to stay there until Li's little device finished doing its job – it couldn't be moved. I figured more soldiers were on the way, and if I was going to be basically immobilized until that thing finished, I needed all the help I could get. So I teleported the soldiers away instead of Gossamer."

He seemed to accept that explanation, and turned to look at Gossamer, who was drinking a bottle of water.

"Look," I said, "we don't know what's going to happen here – how things will shake out. Why don't you tell her how you feel?"

Kane looked at me as if I'd just suggested he take a pig to the prom. "What? You're crazy!" He walked away, shaking his head.

For the first time in a while, as I went into the side room and stretched out on a cot, I thought about Electra and wondered how she was doing. I had to assume she was fine – she had to be. The thought of anything else was unbearable.

MUTATION

Chapter 30

I woke up to the sound of Kane and Gossamer arguing. I walked sleepily out into the main room then out the Exit door to the sub-basement hallway. I'd been told that there was a bathroom out here, so I wandered a little bit until I found it.

After taking some time to freshen up, I returned to our little hideout. Everyone was gathered around Li, who was sitting at the two center tables with the laptop I had swiped. I grabbed a banana from the fruit Kane and Gossamer had picked up on their food run and started eating it.

"Good morning," said Li. "I trust you slept well."

"Well enough," I said. I pointed at the laptop. "Were you able to find out anything?"

Kane and Gossamer exchanged a look but neither said anything.

"It is not good news," Li said. "I am afraid that I am right about the virus. Moreover, telling Dr. Aldiss about my simulations will not induce him to help us."

"Why not?" I asked.

"Because he created the virus," Kane answered.

I almost dropped the food I was holding.

"What???!!!" I screeched.

"He created it," Kane repeated. "According to the information Li pulled off his laptop there."

"He also controls it," Gossamer added.

"What do you mean 'he controls it'?" I asked. "How do you control a virus?"

"This particular virus is a bioengineered construct whose origins are rooted in nanotechnology," Li said. "From a biological standpoint, it acts like an infection.

From a technological stance, it is like a toy that can be controlled remotely."

"So," I said, trying to get a clear understanding, "once it infects someone – attaches to a super's metagene – then Aldiss can control it?"

"More or less," Gavin said, looking nervous.

"This would jibe with the school-as-a-lab theory," Li stated. "And also why some supers have had their powers enhanced, others decreased and some unaffected. He can control the specific virus within each individual super."

"So basically," I said, "he can control all supers with this."

"If they all get infected," Kane said.

"But there is a cure," Li said. "Two cures, actually."

"I'm listening," I said, suddenly all ears.

"According to the information on the laptop, Aldiss has already fashioned a vaccine."

"Can you duplicate it?" I asked.

Li shook his head. "Not in the time we have. Not before everyone succumbs."

"Do we even know that will happen?" Gavin asked, breaking his customary silence. "I mean, he's got a vaccine. What if he plans to distribute it?"

"He doesn't," Kane said.

"Then why create a vaccine?" Gavin asked. "Why make it in the first place if he doesn't plan to use it?"

"Why put brakes on a car?" I asked in response. "You might want to go and go fast, but it doesn't mean you never want to stop."

"I presume," said Li, "that the vaccine is intended to further his control in this situation. He can infect, and he can cure."

There was silence for a few seconds as everyone absorbed this.

"What about the second cure?" I finally asked.

"It is not a cure, per se," Li replied. "It is actually more of a kill switch - a viral self-destruct mechanism. I presume that it is part and parcel of whatever device they use to control the virus."

"Can you build one for us?" I asked. "In the time that we have?"

Li seemed to ponder this for a second. "Possibly, but I don't think we have the proper equipment. The closest we have is vortex technology, but I believe that was all destroyed when Adam broke out."

"Maybe not all of it," I said.

****

It didn't take long to share what I knew. I'd had an interdimensional conference in Magnavolt's office the week before; that meant that there was some sort of vortex technology in there – hopefully some we could use.

"But rather than cannibalize it for this kill switch," Kane asked, "why not use it to call Earth for help? Wouldn't that be faster?"

"The communication interface has been destroyed," Li explained. "We can not call Earth."

Kane still looked perplexed, so I tried to another approach.

"Think of it this way," I said. "With a cell phone, when you make a call, a signal goes out to a cell tower, then gets relayed out to connect to whoever you're trying to reach."

"That is a bit of a simplification–" Li began.

"The point is," I interjected, "you need the tower."

"And our tower's been destroyed," Kane said in understanding.

Li stood up. "I think we should leave as soon as possible. Can you teleport us there?"

"'Us'?" I asked incredulously. "I think I should do this one alone. It's too dangerous."

"Do you know what you are looking for?" Li asked. "What it looks like? What is essential and is not? What you should take and what you can leave?"

I lowered my head in chagrin. Li was absolutely right; if I popped into Magnavolt's conference room, I wouldn't have a clue what I was looking for. Like slipping into the secure wing of the infirmary without knowing the floor plan, my haste was inciting me to make boneheaded mistakes.

"Now that we have settled the matter, when can we leave?" Li asked.

Chapter 31

I popped into Magnavolt's conference room by myself at first, invisible, to make sure it was safe. Not seeing anyone there, I hurriedly returned to our hideout and then teleported both Li and myself back to the conference room.

"There," I said, pointing to the flat screen on the wall, "that's where the others came through for the conference."

Li walked over to the flat screen, then began inspecting it. He looked all around it, then behind it, lifting it gently away from the wall.

"It has a wireless relay," he said, still looking behind the screen.

"What does that mean?" I asked.

"It means that the vortex equipment it used for your conference is not connected directly to it. Otherwise there would be a lot of unsightly wires hanging from the monitor."

"So where is it?"

"Presumably close by, as from what I can tell the relay signal is not very strong." He lowered the screen back to the wall gently, then began methodically searching the room.

I really didn't know what we were looking for (or rather, what it looked like), so I stood back out of the way and glanced around. Despite this being my third visit to this room, it was my first time taking in many of the details. There was a door set in one wall that I hadn't paid attention to before. Some sort of figurine sat in an art niche in the corner. There were also some built-in bookshelves that contained more photos and knickknacks than books. The lower portion of the bookshelves actually consisted of cabinets, and it was when going through these that Li seemed to find what he was looking for.

"Eureka," he said, causing me to come over to look at what he had found.

The cabinets in question were each about two feet in height and width (as well as one foot in depth), and ran the length of the wall of bookshelves. It was in the center cabinet that Li had found what he was looking for.

Looking over his shoulder, I saw what appeared to be a nondescript black box about as large as a loaf of bread. There were a number of colored wires running out of it and connecting to a nearby panel. Unlit diodes dotted its surface. Finally, from what I could see, it appeared to be bolted in place.

"I should get to work," stated Li, producing a toolkit from the folds of his shirt. He had only gotten the first bolt loose when we heard voices coming from the direction of Magnavolt's office.

Li was on his knees at the time, working on getting the vortex equipment out. My initial thought was to teleport Li out of there, but I saw Li shaking his head, as if he knew what I intended. Needless to say, he was right. As he'd said earlier, he was the only person who knew what we needed here.

My next thought was to make him invisible. However, when *I* turn invisible, my own vision automatically switches over to the infrared. A normal person can't see at all when I turn them invisible, and sometimes there are aftereffects, such as not being able to see clearly for a while after becoming visible again. I didn't know Li's power set – had never even asked – so I didn't know what would happen if I made him invisible, but I knew we couldn't afford to have him stumbling around blind.

As the voices got closer, I saw Li scramble to get inside the cabinet with the vortex equipment. I almost laughed – he'd have to be a contortionist to get in there. I glanced at the door for a second as the voices out there suddenly rose in anger. When I looked back, Li was gone, and all I saw was the cabinet door gently closing. I turned invisible just as the voices reached the threshold of the door, and my mouth fell open as I watched them file in.

It was a who's who of my most recent adversaries:
Pace.
Dr. Aldiss.
Estrella.
And Schaefer.

Chapter 32

I silently floated up into the air, listening intently. Not only had the four I mentioned come into the room, but also three armed guards.

"–don't think you're taking this seriously enough," said Aldiss as he and the others entered the conference room. "They've got my laptop, which means they've got the models, the virus schematics, the vaccine formula – everything!"

"Yes," said Pace, taking a seat at the conference table, "but they don't have the resources to do anything with it."

Schaefer took a seat as well. "I agree, Doctor. You're panicking over nothing."

"Easy for you to say," the doctor retorted. "It's not your life's work being lost!"

"Don't be melodramatic," Pace countered. "Everything on that machine is backed up at home."

"Except the data from *this* experiment!" Aldiss cried.

"You didn't get any results that were particularly different than what you got on Earth, so stop whining," Schaefer said. "But if it'll make you happy, maybe instead of killing all these brats I'll use the control module to spare a few for you to take back home as lab rats. Will that satisfy you?"

"It'll be a start," Aldiss said, then left the room.

So, it seemed that Aldiss wasn't the one controlling the virus, or even in charge of the school. It was Schaefer. It almost made my head spin.

No one spoke until they heard Aldiss exit out of the front of Magnavolt's office.

"Should I kill him?" Estrella asked casually.

"No," said Schaefer. "I still need him for this mission. Maybe later."

"What about someone I can kill right now, then?" Estrella asked. "Kid Sensation."

"We've got men scouring the whole school for him and his friends," Pace said. "They're supposed to be somewhere in the sub-basement level, but we haven't been able to locate them."

That was shocking. I had no idea they were so close to finding us. When we got out of here, we'd probably need to find another clubhouse to hang out in.

"Look, I took this assignment because you told me I could get my hands on Kid Sensation," she said.

"No," Pace corrected, "you took this assignment because we threw a boatload of money at you to do it. Kid Sensation was just a bonus."

"Whatever," Estrella said. "I owe him for what he did to my brother. And he's supposed to be *here*!"

The way she emphasized the last word sent a chill up my spine. Did she mean *here*, in this room?

There was an unexpected squeak, like the sound of a rusty hinge on a door.

"What was that?" Schaefer asked, as he and his companions, as well as the guards in the room, looked around uncertainly.

It seemed to have come from the cabinet where Li was. Rather than sitting quietly, he must have still been trying to get the vortex equipment loose, although I don't know how he was managing in such a tight space.

Pace seemed to figure out the source of the noise first. He snapped his fingers to get the attention of the guards, then pointed at the cabinets. Pace and Schaefer quietly got up and moved away from the conference table as the guards, weapons cocked, started converging on the cabinets. In a split second, I made my decision.

I turned visible and dropped down to the floor at the back of the room.

"You looking for me?" I asked as all eyes turned in my direction.

I phased as the guards opened fire, and ran along the wall opposite the cabinets in order to keep Li out of the line of fire. I ran out of the room with everyone in hot pursuit.

I hadn't shifted into super speed, as the goal wasn't to try to get away. My intent was merely to get them out of Magnavolt's conference room so Li could finish his work. With that in mind, I led them – and other guards who joined in – on a merry chase through the school hallways. Occasionally Estrella would teleport ahead of me, lasers blasting, but she didn't seem to realize that I was phased and couldn't be hit.

After about five minutes, I figured Li had had enough time, so I cut around a corner and teleported back to the conference room. When I popped in, Li was nowhere in sight. However, the vortex equipment was gone, too, so that was a good sign. Still, with everyone in the hallways looking for me, he'd have a tough time getting back to the sub-basement. I needed to find him.

I slipped out of the conference room, then quietly exited Magnavolt's office. No one seemed to be around. Still, I practically tiptoed down the hallway with my back to the wall, keeping my eyes peeled for any sign of the way Li might have gone. I was so wrapped up in my own thoughts that I almost stepped in a small puddle of reddish goo on the floor.

MUTATION

At first I thought it might be blood, but upon closer inspection I realized that it wasn't. It seemed to be some kind of industrial lubricant or hydraulic fluid. Now that I was paying attention, I could see droplets of it every few feet, heading away from me, like someone had randomly been squeezing it out of a sponge as they walked.

Trusting my instincts, I shifted into super speed and followed the drops. They led away from the direction that everyone had been chasing me, down a different hallway towards a back stairwell.

I stopped when I reached the stairwell door and listened for a few seconds. I couldn't hear anything, so – deeming it safe – I phased and went through the door.

Li was sitting on the floor, looking drained. Tucked under one arm he had the vortex equipment. Next to him were two unconscious security guards. I grinned at him, impressed that he had taken out two armed men. Then I saw the hole in his shirt, near the area where his heart would be.

It was undoubtedly a bullet hole, but it wasn't bleeding. Instead, it was leaking the fluid that I had seen earlier. I telescoped my vision and looked closely at the wound. Rather than jagged and torn tissue, I saw sparks and wires, many of the latter connected to a rectangular piece of white ceramic with flashing lights.

"You're a robot!" I said in surprise. Now so much made sense – his stilted manner of speech, his advanced expertise in science and technology, etc.

"Technically, I am an android," he replied. He began struggling to his feet and I gave him a hand.

"Are you okay?" I asked.

"For the nonce. As long as my core processor is not damaged beyond repair I can recover, although the bullet did come close. Still, I could use a moment to tend to my wounds. Can you take us somewhere appropriate – somewhere other than our base of operations?"

"Did you have a particular place in mind?"

He did, in fact, and when he told me I smiled, because I should have thought of it myself.

****

I teleported us to the combat training room. As Li had assumed, the place was deserted. The various robots were in shutdown mode, since no one was actually using the facility. Li headed straight for a small workroom near the back of the combat area, where damaged robots were brought for repair. He didn't ask for my help and I thought enough of him to let him have some privacy.

After about half an hour he came out, looking much like his old self. The hole was still in his shirt, but the "flesh" underneath looked essentially whole.

"Everything good?" I asked.

"Yes," he said. "I am fully functional again for all intents and purposes."

"Okay, let's get back."

"If I might ask a favor first," Li said, touching my arm. "I would greatly appreciate the others not knowing about my…distinctiveness. It might anger them to learn they have been taking direction from a machine."

"Understood," I said, then teleported us back to the sub-basement.

MUTATION

Chapter 33

Li went to work on the vortex equipment almost as soon as we arrived, while I debriefed the rest of the troops. It didn't take long.

"So they were waiting for you?" Gossamer asked.

"Yep," I answered, "like they knew we were coming, except we were already there when they showed up."

"But that doesn't make any sense," said Kane. "Unless they're psychic or something."

Rudi suddenly sprang to mind, and it occurred to me that she could possibly be here as well. Then I dismissed the notion.

"No, I've encountered one of the psychics they use before," I said, "and if it were her, they'd be breaking down the door right now."

"But you said they knew that we were in the sub-basement," Gavin said.

"Yes, but they can't seem to find us for some reason," I added.

Kane and Gossamer exchanged glances, simultaneously grinned, and then high-fived each other. That was the largest display of solidarity I'd seen from them.

"What?" I asked.

"There's a glamour on this entire section of the sub-basement," Gossamer said, smiling mischievously. "Kane and I cast it jointly when we first set up down here."

"For anyone looking," Kane added, "the hallways and stairs that lead to this area all look and feel like dead ends."

MUTATION

Gossamer and Kane started chatting animatedly about how well their glamour must be working, and I used the opportunity to go grab a couple of apples from the fridge. Gavin, ever the loner, went to the workstation and sat down.

I felt a little sorry for him. Gavin hadn't really been involved in any of the missions and there really wasn't a strong effort to draw him out during conversations. He was here more by virtue of the fact that he was immune to the virus than anything else. As Li had said, he seemed socially awkward, but that didn't mean I couldn't be friendly. I walked towards where he was sitting.

I didn't necessarily come up behind him quietly; I think he was just so focused on the computer screen that he didn't notice me. For a second, I watched reams of data flying by on the screen he was looking at. It seemed impossible that he could read that fast, but then I remembered Li mentioning that his power let him connect directly to computers. I tapped him on the shoulder to get his attention, preparing to just make simple conversation.

He glanced over his shoulder, but when he saw it was me, he jumped to his feet so fast that he knocked over the chair he'd been sitting in. He seemed to almost cringe, backing himself towards the tiny corner between the edge of the workstation and the wall. Moreover, I was picking up not just unease or discomfort from him, but something verging on terror.

"Y-y-yes?" he stammered.

"I just wanted to see how you were doing," I said. "We really haven't had a chance to talk, so I just figured now was a good time."

"Actually," he said, "I'm kind of in the middle of something. Maybe later?"

I nodded. "Okay. That sounds fine." I walked away towards the couch and sat down while Gavin picked up the chair he'd knocked over and gingerly sat down, keeping an eye on me all the while.

I finished the apples and then went to the fridge for a bottle of water. As I twisted the top off and leaned against the wall, I glanced around at our little group and couldn't help thinking what an odd little band we were.

Li, an android.

Gossamer, an elf.

Kane, a plain old, regular human with magic.

Me, basically a mongrel with alien genes.

Gavin, a super who connected to computers.

Now that I thought about it, Gavin was really the only true, pure meta among us. The rest of us just got lumped in the same category because of the things we could do.

And just like that, the clouds in my mind parted and the answer came to me like a divine revelation. It was so startling that I jerked up from the position I'd been in, leaning against the wall, like something had bitten me.

Li had noticed the movement. "Is something wrong, Jim?"

"As a matter of fact, there is," I acknowledged as I walked over to where he was sitting at the center tables. "Gavin, can you come here for a second?" I shouted across the room.

Gavin looked over nervously, then slowly got up and walked towards us. Gossamer and Kane, who had been talking over by the Exit door, joined us as well.

MUTATION

Gavin stopped when he reached the center tables. As usual, he had positioned himself in such a way as to keep as much distance as possible between him and me. It only confirmed what I was thinking.

"Yes?" Gavin said quizzically.

"I just wanted to ask you something," I said. "Why aren't you sick?"

Chapter 34

Gavin looked like someone had handed him a scorpion.

"What???!!!" he asked.

"Why aren't you sick?" I repeated. "Why don't you have the virus, like all the other metas in this school?"

"I-I-I-I'm immune," he stammered. "Like the rest of you guys."

"No, no, no, no, no," I said. "You're not immune."

"What do you mean?" asked Kane. "Is he sick?"

"No, he isn't," I said. "And that's the problem."

"You're going to have to explain," said Gossamer.

"Fine," I said adamantly, not taking my eyes off Gavin. "The virus attaches to the metagene. Gossamer's not sick because she's an elf. She's not human. Ergo, she doesn't have a metagene.

"Kane is a human practitioner of magic. However, none of his abilities arise genetically because he doesn't have the metagene. Therefore, he's not sick.

"I'm not immune, but I am a biological anomaly to a certain extent, and my body fought off the infection.

"Li," I said, hesitating, not sure how to say it, "also has a unique physiology so that he isn't susceptible to disease. So he's not sick.

"That just leaves you, Gavin. A regular super with the metagene, just like all the other infected students here. So I ask again, why aren't you sick?"

I felt confident in my analysis, but to an extent I was bluffing. I didn't really have any proof of what I was implying, just random data and circumstantial evidence -

like the fact that Gavin practically ran away every time I got near him, as if he were scared I'd infect him.

That being the case, I half expected Gavin to laugh it off and call me crazy. I wouldn't have been at all surprised if he had hotly denied everything, declared I'd besmirched his honor and challenged me to a duel at twenty paces.

But none of that happened.

Instead, Gavin started crying.

****

Apparently Gavin's parents had been dissidents in some Third-World country ruled by a harsh dictator. They had been granted political asylum twenty years ago. Gray was now threatening to deport them, send them back to their home country - along with Gavin's brother and sister - where they would all likely face execution.

"When did he recruit you?" I asked.

"About a year ago," Gavin replied, "when I was first accepted to the Academy."

"A year!" Gossamer screamed. Face twisted into a snarl, she drew her daggers, wanting to take his head off. While Kane physically restrained her, she spouted off a stream of elvish that I am quite sure had nothing but four-letter equivalents in English.

"And the virus?" Li asked.

"They gave vials of it to me right before I came back this year," Gavin said, hanging his head.

"How did you introduce it into the student population?" Li asked.

"The water system, for most of them," he replied.

"Of course." Li nodded in understanding, then began explaining after noting my confused look. "Each dorm has its own water supply system. The dorm for the boys, the one for the girls, the housing for faculty and staff. The main pumps are located in the basement below each building."

"So all he had to do was insert the virus into the tanks he was interested in and leave everything else alone," I said.

"Like the faculty and staff," Li said. "The control group."

Gavin just nodded.

"Hold on, you said you used the water system to infect 'most' of the students," I noted. "Who didn't get infected that way?"

Gavin looked me in the eye. "You."

I frowned, then remembered. "The cup you gave me. The cup at the lake."

"Yeah," Gavin admitted. "The guy in charge over here, Schaefer, he's got a real thing for you. I mean, he wants you dead. He personally came to me and told me he wanted you infected first, and he wanted you to have a double dose."

"Wait a minute," I said. "All that was before I got sick – before we allegedly sent for Aldiss and the CDC guys. When did he get here?"

Gavin made a derisive sound. "They go back and forth all the time! They've got their own vortex technology. Sometimes they mask the dimensional signature by traveling at the same time that you guys have a gate open here, but they've got free rein in that department. That's how they could afford to blow the vortex gate at the school here. They've got their own way back home!"

"*They* blew they gate?" Kane asked, having calmed Gossamer down. "They said Adam did it!"

"They say a lot of stuff!" Gavin shouted back.

"So how much have you told them?" I asked. "About us and what we're trying to do?"

Gavin lowered his head.

"Jeez!" Kane cried. "He's told them everything! All the time we thought he was on the computer playing games, he was spilling his guts!"

"That certainly explains how they knew when we were after the modeling software," Li said. "And when we were coming to the conference room in Magnavolt's office."

"But they were late getting there both times," I said. "What's the story there?"

"I don't know," Gavin sighed. "The messages got held up somehow, like they hit some kind of wall. I guess Kane and Gossamer's glamour acted like some kind of barrier or speed bump."

"So, what's their plan now?" Gossamer asked.

"I don't know," Gavin said.

Gossamer pulled her right blade out and put it to his throat.

"I don't know!" Gavin wailed. "Please! I don't know! All I know is that something's happening on the other side - back on Earth - so they're calling an abort."

"What?!" I yelled. "When?"

"Right now," Gavin answered. "That's what I was reading when you first came over and tapped me on the shoulder."

"So they're just going to leave?" asked Kane. "Just give up and leave us here after all this trouble they've gone through? What do they think will happen when we tell people back home what happened?"

"You don't understand," Gavin said. "Schaefer's going to fully activate everyone's metagene – even the dormant ones – before they leave. There won't be anybody left to say anything."

"What are you talking about?" Gossamer interjected. "There will still be us, if no one else."

Gavin shook his head. "There are at least two dozen students here with a power level equal to Adam Atom's when their metagene is cranked all the way up. At least five of them might have the power to split the planet. This school – maybe this whole world – will be a smoking pile of rubble by the time anyone else from Earth gets here."

MUTATION

Chapter 35

I spent about two minutes randomly teleporting to different areas of the school before returning to our hideout.

"He's right," I said of Gavin, "they all seem to have pulled out. No guards, no CDC, no Estrella, no Schaefer."

"How'd they move out so fast?" Kane asked.

I shrugged. "Probably Estrella. She's a teleporter."

"So why is *he* still here?" asked Gossamer, nodding in Gavin's direction.

It was an excellent question. I turned to Gavin, who sat morosely in his chair, eyes red from crying, and asked him.

"Pace and Schaefer mentioned something before about tying up loose ends when they finished here," Gavin said after a moment. "It didn't sound like they were talking about paperwork, and as far as I can tell, I'm a loose end."

"And you still kept helping them?" Kane asked. "Even though they were going to kill you?"

"They have a noose around my family's neck!" Gavin screamed. "I had to help them! And it doesn't matter anyway - I'm dead if I go with them, I'm dead if I stay with you! I'm dead, dead, dead!!!"

Gavin dropped his head into his hands and started crying again. We went back to trying to figure something out.

"So what now?" asked Gossamer.

"We need to find out where they went," I said. "Right now, they've got the only bus pass home."

I looked at Gavin, who was still sobbing. Li followed my glance.

"He insists he does not know where they are," Li said. "He states that they did not tell him where they set up their vortex gate."

"And the full campus – including all the replicas of residential areas, warehouse districts, and so on – is the size of a city," Kane said. "They could be anywhere, setting up their vortex to leave right now."

The mention of the vortex brought an earlier conversation to mind.

"Gavin," I said, turning to him, "you mentioned something earlier about Schaefer and his crew coming over at the same time we did."

Gavin looked up, eyes puffy, and nodded. "Every vortex creates an energy signature. Traveling at the same time as you guys allowed them to mask theirs within the one created here."

"Well, we don't have a vortex for them to hide their signature in now," I said. "What's changed?"

"They've continued to work on improving the vortex technology over the past few years," Gavin said. "The supers haven't. And they had a breakthrough recently, so now, I think they know how to effectively keep their comings and goings secret."

"We have to locate their vortex gate," Li said, "or we are doomed."

"How?" Kane asked. "We don't have a clue where to start looking."

I smiled. "Maybe we do."

Then I told them what I'd seen on my trip through the vortex.

MUTATION

I had thought Aldiss looked familiar. Now that all the pieces of the puzzle were in front of me, I knew why: he had been one of the people I'd seen traveling through the other vortex tunnel.

I told Li and the others what I'd seen through the vortex gate that Aldiss and his people had been going through: the letters *A-K-A* in a window of the building.

"Of course," I said, reflecting back, "the *K* had been backwards."

"Understood," said Li. "The letters were painted on the other side of the window."

We were in Magnavolt's office, with Li sitting at the principal's computer and the rest of us – *sans* Gavin (who was in the bullet-riddled conference room) – huddled around him. With all the bad guys gone, there was no need to stay down in the sub-basement.

At the moment, Li was pulling up a list of all the areas of campus that used real-world replicas for training. Although what I had seen had the appearance of a business, Li was pulling up residential listings as well as commercial and industrial.

"I am sorry," he said. "There is nothing containing the letters *A-K-A*. Are you certain that is what you saw?"

"I'm positive," I said. Still, I closed my eyes, concentrated. I could see the guys moving through the tunnel, including Aldiss...the equipment they had...the room they were headed into. There was the window, the letters, the broken glass...

My eyes snapped open. I started pulling open the drawers of Magnavolt's desk, maniacally looking for what I needed.

"What are you looking for, Jim?" asked Gossamer. "Can we help?"

I didn't answer, just kept looking until I found it in the bottom of the left-hand drawer: a pen and pad of paper. I put the pad on the desk and drew a large letter R on it. I put my hand over the top part of the R.

"Imagine that the top part of the R is gone," I said, "from the vertical line on the left to just before it curves into the loop on the right. Does that look like a K to you?"

"Sort of," said Kane. "I mean, if you're in a hurry and glance at it, you could mistake it for a K."

"Well, when I saw the window in the vortex, some of the glass was broken out," I said, "including a piece near the top of what I thought was K. I think it wasn't a K but an R instead."

Li could already see where I was going with it and had revised the search before I even finished speaking.

"One item shows up with the letters A-R-A," he announced. "Manny's Garage."

Chapter 36

Li was able to pull up a layout of the campus, so we knew where to find Manny's Garage. However, there were still only four of us (five if you counted Gavin, although I don't think anybody felt we could at that point). That was a small number to pit against a bunch of armed men, not to mention Estrella.

Recruiting other students was out, for the same reasons as before: they still had the virus and were still unstable.

"What about the faculty and staff?" Kane suggested.

In all our planning, we had practically forgotten about the so-called control group.

"They won't be able to help you," Gavin said from the doorway of the conference room. Apparently he was tired of being ostracized.

"Why not?" asked Li.

"Because they're all sedated," Gavin answered. "Aldiss told them that he needed to inoculate them against the virus, but instead he gave them sedatives – knocked them out. They've been getting regular rounds of sedatives since and are being kept in the nullifier section just in case one of them wakes up."

"That's just great," said Kane. "So it's just the four of us."

"Maybe not," I said, glancing in Gavin's direction. We needed every soldier we could get in this army.

Empathically, I opened myself up fully. I needed to read this right. "Gavin, your friends have deserted you. In fact, they want you dead. You can stay loyal to them and stand by while a bunch of innocent kids meet their maker, or you can do something about it. And let's be clear, even if you make the right choice here, I can't promise what will happen to you later. But you need to decide right now. Will you keep supporting them, or will you stand with us?"

As I spoke, I felt a deep swirl of emotions within Gavin. Self-loathing, anger, fear, desperation, and more, but when he answered, I felt determination and – most of all – sincerity.

"I'm with you," he said.

****

Our plan was more than a little bold. Basically, we needed Schaefer's vortex gate. I felt that if I could eyeball it, I could teleport the entire thing back to the Academy – where our old gate was located – and we could fire it up. Li vetoed the idea.

"I do not mean to say that it would not work," he said, "but it would be a massive undertaking in the sense of getting everything properly connected and positioned, reconfiguring the spatial coordinates for the new location, performing an initial–"

"Got it," I said. "It's impractical and takes up time we don't have. What do you propose then?"

"I can reconfigure the coordinates for the vortex," Li replied, "so that while the gate stays where it is, the actual vortex opens and exits elsewhere."

"Is that possible?" asked Gossamer.

"Absolutely," said Gavin, speaking up now that he was once more a part of the group. "It's how we sometimes get here by plane. The vortex machinery isn't on the aircraft; it's on the ground. The vortex just opens in the air."

"And if we can get all the students through the vortex quickly enough," Li said, "they may be out of range when the virus is activated."

"That's our plan, then," I said.

Chapter 37

Gavin got what was probably the easiest task: get everybody in the school to the destroyed vortex gate. Of course, there were sub-tasks involved, which included getting the faculty and staff out of the nullifiers, getting the rest of the students organized, etc. Still, he was able to get started on his job at least an hour before the rest of us as we made our plans to infiltrate Manny's Garage.

Needless to say, I couldn't teleport us there. Other than what I had glimpsed from inside the vortex, I had never seen the place. Moreover, we didn't know what kind of reception would be awaiting us. That said, I could get us fairly close.

We had a map of the garage's location, so I knew the direction we needed to head in. I looked that way and telescoped my vision. A residential area came into view; I teleported us to the backyard of a small house there. Looking again in the proper direction, I could now see Manny's Garage. It sat in an area around other skilled trades such as plumbing and electrical shops, on a street that ran north-south.

Outside of Manny's, I noticed quite a number of armed guards milling around. I watched for a few minutes, but didn't see any patrols. In fact, the guards appeared downright disengaged, as if they were merely biding time. They obviously knew they were leaving and were probably anxious to do so. No one wanted to wander too far and get stranded (and Schaefer didn't strike me as a no-man-left-behind type of guy).

I didn't see any of the bigwigs – Pace, Aldiss, Estrella, or Schaefer. That meant that they were probably inside. I teleported us to the back side of an ancient, crumbling warehouse a few blocks away from the garage.

Everyone knew their roles. Kane and Gossamer were to draw off as many of the guards as possible. Li and I would then slip inside, where he would alter the vortex coordinates (although he felt he could also handle Pace, Aldiss, and Schaefer, if necessary). My job was to engage Estrella; with her suite of powers, I was the only one who could.

Gossamer and Kane wished us luck, then took off towards the north end of the warehouse. Li and I went in the other direction. Then we crept over furtively, block by block, towards the garage. Stealth probably wasn't necessary, however; the guards I'd seen earlier didn't even have anyone on watch. (They probably thought we had no way to find them.)

After a few minutes, we found ourselves on the south-facing wall of a building that sat on the same street as Manny's Garage. Peeking around the corner, I saw the guards in pretty much the same position as before. I checked my watch; we had about two minutes to kill – enough time for a little recon.

"Wait here," I said to Li. I went invisible, then flew down the street to the garage. Phasing in through the window, I saw a huge workspace - at least twenty thousand square feet in size. There were a number of cars parked willy-nilly throughout the place, a few other vehicles under tarps, and a station wagon hoisted up on a hydraulic lift. A large industrial magnet hung down from the ceiling at the south end of the roof. Finally, there was a long row of windows - running almost the length of the building - with the words "MANNY'S GARAGE" painted on them in large letters. (I took a certain amount of pride in noting that some of the glass was broken out of the windows, including the top portion of the R in the word "garage.")

The vortex gate was set up against one of the walls, next to a copious amount of hi-tech machinery. A group of three men who I assumed to be technicians were checking the equipment, apparently prepping the gate for activation. A small crowd of about a dozen men and women in lab coats - clearly the CDC team - stood near the middle of the room, chatting amiably and trying to stay out of the way of the technicians. Near the back of the room were a couple of supervisor offices, one of which had a glass window (presumably to let the boss keep an eye on things in the shop). Pace, Estrella, Aldiss, and Schaefer were in there now.

Schaefer was sitting behind the only desk in the room, speaking while fiddling around inside a briefcase in front of him. The others stood, facing him. I flew over and phased through the wall, staying above the room's occupants.

"-derstand what your problem is," Schaefer was saying. "Dead is dead."

"I wanted to do it myself!" shouted Estrella, white light pulsing angrily around her.

"So did I," said Schaefer, "but you don't see me crying about it."

I didn't need three guesses to figure out who they were talking about.

"Look," Pace said to Estrella, playing peacemaker, "you wanted Kid Sensation dead, and he'll *be* dead. And by being part of this, you're bringing it about. In that sense, you *are* killing him."

226

Estrella wasn't buying it. "There's no satisfaction in this! I wanted to look into his eyes when it happened. I wanted him to know that it was me, that I was the cause of his death. But this? We're running away like rats!"

"Rats survive," said Pace. "And we can't afford to be here any longer. It might even be too late right now."

Aldiss went a little pale at that. Estrella merely stormed out of the room.

"Done," announced Schaefer. He turned to Aldiss. "Now, Doctor, are you sure there's no way to override the fifteen-minute delay?"

Aldiss shook his head. "No, the tech who handled that portion was Morton. He built in the delay just in case the person pushing the button changed his mind."

"Change my mind about killing supers?" Schaefer asked rhetorically. "Unlikely. Supers killed my family." He stared off into space for a second before continuing. "Anyway, where's Morton now?"

"I believe you had him shot," said Aldiss.

Schaefer looked at Pace, who confirmed. "You did."

"Hmmm...tough break," said Schaefer, looking unbothered. Then he stood up. "Well, gentlemen, we have a quarter of an hour to get off this rock." Then he left the room, leaving the open briefcase on the desk.

Pace started to follow, but Aldiss grabbed his arm.

"He's insane," said Aldiss. "You do know that?"

"People could say the same of you, Doctor," replied Pace, smiling. "Especially in light of this monster virus you designed."

"I was only trying to explore the boundaries of science. He's beyond that. His need for revenge almost got us killed!"

"You mean Adam Atom? Yes, he probably did go overboard on that kid, exciting his metagene like that. But if that kind of thing bothers you, maybe - in addition to a delay before full activation - you guys should also have equipped the control module with an abort option. Oh wait - Morton was working on that when Schaefer had him shot. Too bad; without an abort switch, once the button is pressed, it can't be stopped. The metagene of every infected super will go haywire soon."

I almost screamed. I swooped down and looked at the open briefcase Schaefer had left on the desk. There was a complex computer device inside, with a monitor and keyboard. The screen displayed a countdown.

13:44

13:43

13:42

Even worse, there was a flashing message that stated "Kill Switch Overridden." In short, the kill switch couldn't be activated, and - based on Pace's statements - there was no way to abort the countdown.

"Please!" Aldiss was saying. "You've been the voice of reason this entire mission. That's why you're here, isn't it? To keep that madman under control. That's why you're the one who usually does all the talking, because anyone hearing him speak would know he's crazy inside two minutes!"

"Doctor, I like you," Pace said, placing his hands on the man's shoulders, "but you should be very aware of the acoustics when you raise your voice like that. You never know who might hear you."

If possible, Aldiss became paler than before. I teleported back to Li.

"Were you able to learn anything?" he asked.

"Yeah," I said. "We're further up the creek than we thought."

I explained to him about the countdown. He just nodded, without saying anything. Then we stood silently, waiting for the signal.

Come on...come on.

Suddenly, there was a sound like a muffled explosion from the north end of the street - presumably the distraction created by Kane and Gossamer. The guards all came to attention, weapons ready. Then one of the guards went down with a grunt, and the rest opened fire towards that end of the street, shooting indiscriminately. That was my cue.

I shapeshifted into Schaefer and appeared behind the rearmost guard in the group. I clearly wasn't dressed as Schaefer was, but people tend to notice the face and not the clothes. I hoped that was true in this case as I tapped the guard on the shoulder. Startled, he stopped firing, but I saw recognition in his eyes when he looked at me.

"What are you waiting for???!!" I screamed, spewing spittle in his face. "Go after them!!!"

"Yes, sir!" the guard acknowledged, wiping his face. Then he screamed and went charging towards the north end of the street.

"All of you!" I shouted, and several more guards turned to look at me. "Go! Go! Go!"

A few seconds later, they were all running down the street, firing.

I looked behind me, where Li had stepped out from hiding. Knowing that we were on a tight time schedule, I took a chance and teleported us both to the office inside the garage. My hunch had been right; everyone was racing over to the side of the garage facing the street to find out what all the commotion was about, letting us arrive unnoticed. I pushed Li down out of sight and turned invisible.

"That's just great," I muttered sarcastically. "They're not leaving! I was hoping they'd all run outside but most are just looking out the windows."

"Perhaps you could provide some incentive," Li said. I looked at him to see what he was talking about and saw him holding out a handgun in my direction.

"Where did you get that?" I asked, reaching to take the gun.

"I removed it from one of the guards you found me with in the stairwell earlier."

"Way to think ahead," I said. "Get ready; here we go."

I teleported Li down by the vortex equipment, then became visible and stepped out of the office. Everyone's back was to me. I screamed and began firing over the heads of the crowd, into the windows of the garage.

I only fired a couple of shots, but the sound was deafening in the enclosed space. People began screaming and running for the exits - including Pace and Aldiss – as glass rained down around them. The only person who stood their ground was Estrella, light shimmering around her. It occurred to me then that I hadn't seen Schaefer, but I didn't have time to dwell on it.

"There's my date," Estrella said, grinning mischievously. "I was afraid you were going to stand me up."

From where she was positioned, I didn't think Estrella could see Li (there was a tarp-covered vehicle shielding him from her view) and I needed to keep it that way. I shifted into super speed and charged her.

Unlike our previous encounter, there was no one here to predict my moves or make her insubstantial. I caught her in the midsection with my shoulder, then slammed her into a wall.

At super speed, I rarely ever hit anything with my bare hand; it's a good way to end up with broken bones. Some speedsters don't care, though; they're so hopped up on adrenaline that they don't feel the pain, and their metabolisms are so high that they heal almost immediately. I didn't feel like testing that theory, and I was in no position to deal with a broken hand, so – while it may not sound gallant – I pistol-whipped Estrella with the gun I was still holding. Then again. And a third time.

Before I could get a fourth turn at bat, she vanished. She had obviously teleported, and my first thought was to check on Li. I'd barely turned my head in his direction when a crushing weight fell on me. Estrella had teleported above me.

Her weight bore me down to the ground, where she cupped my head in her hands, lifted and then smashed it against the concrete floor. I immediately saw stars, feeling as if someone had just put my skull in a car compactor. I tore a page out of her playbook and teleported.

I didn't go far, just a few feet away. I needed to keep her preoccupied so that Li could finish. I raised the

231

gun and fired as she turned in my direction. The light around her body intensified and the bullets seemed to dissolve. At the same time, I became violently ill. I clutched my stomach, doubled over, and threw up.

I was still heaving when Estrella appeared beside me. She kneed me in the face, a move that sent me soaring backwards before landing hard enough to knock the wind out of me and crack my skull on the floor again. Two things happened almost simultaneously then.

First, a jagged red line appeared in the air behind Estrella. I recognized it as the spatial scar I'd first seen in my dorm room. Then Gossamer and Kane stepped through it.

At the same time, I heard gunfire coming from Li's direction. I painfully lifted my head from the floor and looked in his direction. Schaefer was there, holding what appeared to be a shotgun. He fired, sending Li staggering back in my direction. A second shot knocked him off his feet. From where I was, it appeared that the shots had severely damaged Li's stomach and the left side of his face. Li didn't move.

I struggled to my hands and knees, head spinning. When I tried to rise, nausea hit me like a tsunami and I collapsed back down. At this point, Gossamer and Kane were taking on Estrella. Gossamer had her daggers crossed in front of her, forming her shield as Estrella fired a laser at her. Kane, standing diagonal to Estrella, fired a sphere of light at her, but she teleported, appearing next to him. She gripped his wrists, and suddenly the air was filled with Kane's anguished screams and the smell of cooking flesh. Then she flung him to the side like a toy, sending him crashing into the door of a nearby SUV.

Kane flopped over onto the ground like a dead chicken and didn't move.

Over by Li, Schaefer was reloading, muttering something about "freaking robot." Unexpectedly, Li moved. His arm swung in a wide arc, sweeping Schaefer's legs out from under him. Schaefer hit the ground with a bone-jarring thud. Li stood up, wires and circuitry exposed, then bent over, grabbed Schaefer by the shirt, and flung him into the wall. Schaefer hit hard enough to crack the plaster, then fell down to the floor, out of sight, behind one of the cars. Li went back to work on the vortex equipment.

Near me, Gossamer was fighting Estrella, trying to get at her with her daggers, but it was a lost cause. She knew she couldn't win, but she fought anyway. She spared a second to give me a concerned glance, and that's when I realized that Gossamer wasn't trying to win. She was simply trying to buy time. For me. Because I was the only one who could really face Estrella. With that in mind, I focused - trying to take control of all my bodily functions to combat the nausea, despite my throbbing head - and struggled to my feet.

Estrella teleported behind Gossamer, firing lasers at the elf's hands. Gossamer's daggers went flying. Estrella gripped Gossamer by her hair, twisting the latter's head until they were almost face to face.

Oddly enough, I was still holding the gun. I hadn't fully conquered the nausea, but I raised the weapon and fired. I couldn't tell if any hit Estrella, but she just laughed.

"Don't you get it?" she asked, chuckling. "I'm a star, like the sun! You can't kill a star!"

Her words triggered something in my brain, something I tried to remember – a conversation of some sort. Without warning, it came to me. I forgot about my nausea and concentrated on a new train of thought.

Estrella turned her attention back to Gossamer. "As for you, girlfriend, you hit me in the face with my own laser before. And I just happen to believe in an eye for an eye…"

Estrella pointed a finger at the right side of Gossamer's face and made a downstroke motion. Gossamer screamed, her body convulsing almost spasmodically.

"And now the other one," Estrella said. She raised her hand, then stopped. She looked in my direction with a curious expression, then let go of Gossamer (who collapsed to the floor) and placed a hand to her chest, gasping. I kept concentrating, staying focused since my plan seemed to be working. Forgotten, Gossamer crawled slowly across the floor towards Kane, who was just coming to.

Estrella raised a trembling hand at me. "What are you doing???!!!" she screamed. She fired a laser at me, but her hand was shaking so badly that she missed. (Which is a good thing, because I was focusing so hard that I forgot to become insubstantial.)

"Stop it!" she screamed. "*Stop it!!!*"

My phasing power actually had several components. I could make things insubstantial, so they could pass through solid objects like ghosts; I could also return them to their normal state. In addition, I could make physical objects *more* substantial – increasing their weight and density beyond what was natural for them. I had never done the latter with anything or anyone other than myself, but I was doing it now to Estrella. If BT's theory was right, she could be made to collapse under her own weight and density – two elements which I was now increasing substantially.

Estrella lifted her head up and let out an ear-splitting, undulating scream that shattered the remaining glass in the window. Then she vanished.

Gossamer and Kane were now huddled together. Gossamer sported an unsightly wound that went from just above the middle of her right eyebrow, across her eye, and almost straight down to the middle of her cheek. I couldn't see her eye itself – the lid seemed soldered shut – but it could not be good. Kane's wrists looked ugly and charred, like barbecue left on the grill too long.

The sound of a ricochet near my feet made me instinctively crouch. It had come from near the vortex equipment. When I looked in that direction, I saw Schaefer – bloodied and with a crazed look in his eye – on the far side of Li, firing an assault rifle wildly.

"Get out!" I shouted at Gossamer and Kane, who had just gotten to their feet. They didn't wait to be told twice. Gossamer raised a glowing hand and her daggers flew to her, and then they scrambled out the door.

Down by Li, I saw the vortex gate light up. Any second now, if Li knew what he was doing, the vortex tunnel at the Academy should open. We had to leave.

Schaefer was still firing when Li stood up and rushed him. Despite the damage he'd taken from the shotgun, Li still appeared to be very much functional. He had almost reached Schaefer when suddenly his momentum was checked and he flew up into the air, limbs flailing. He hit a large circular object up near the roof with an echoing metallic thud.

It was the industrial magnet. Schaefer had turned it on and positioned it to trap Li, who was struggling to get free. Schaefer pointed his rifle up and fired repeatedly, ripping Li to shreds.

I ran towards him, determined to help. Schaefer saw me coming and dropped the rifle. He held his hands up at chest level to show me what he was gripping: a hand grenade.

"That's far enough," he said, when I got close. "I don't know what your little robot buddy was doing, but one more step and I'll erase all his efforts."

I was about to mention that destroying the vortex would leave him stranded here, too, but from what I could sense of his emotions, he was beyond caring about stuff like that. In fact, I could feel an utter, black hate in him, and it was directed at me.

I backed up slowly, then found my movement checked by the hydraulic lift. Up above me was the station wagon I'd seen earlier.

A look of pure evil came over Schaefer's face. I knew what he was going to do before he even did it. He pulled the pin, then tossed the grenade at me. I phased, and the grenade passed through me, striking the lift before falling to the ground.

I turned my head to the side as the grenade exploded, destroying the base of the lift and cracking the concrete floor. Dust flew up into the air as if caught in a windstorm. There was the unmistakable screech of tearing metal as the lift slowly tilted and then fell forward in Schaefer's direction. I thought that it would hit him, but instead it struck the ground about three feet in front of him, embedding itself in the floor.

The station wagon that was on the lift, however, thudded to the ground grill-first, headlights shattering and hood crumpling. Then it slowly fell forward onto its roof, crushing a shrieking Schaefer under it.

I didn't bother checking on him. Instead, I looked to see if the vortex equipment was damaged. There were a few sparks, but in truth I didn't know enough about the technology to determine if it was still in working order. My thoughts on the subject were interrupted by someone shouting my name.

"Jim!" Kane screamed from the doorway. "Come quick! There's some kind of red giant out here!"

Red giant? I wasn't sure that I'd heard him right. I ran outside and saw something I'd never seen before.

Lumbering in our direction from the far north end of the street was a woman. She was red all over - not just her complexion but also the soft light that surrounded her - roughly twelve feet tall, and just as big around. As Kane had said, a red giant. As she came waddling slowly down the street, wailing at the top of her lungs, buildings on both sides seemed to crumble inwards. With a shock, I realized that the woman was Estrella. Whatever was happening to her was running its course at a high rate of speed. In addition, it was affecting the environment, because in the few seconds I'd been outside, the wind had whipped up into a frenzy, blowing in Estrella's direction.

"You have to get us out of here!" Kane shouted, Gossamer leaning protectively against him.

"Me?" I asked incredulously. "How?"

"Teleport us!"

"Teleport?" I asked, puzzled by what he meant. The word *sounded* familiar...my head was still throbbing, making it hard to think.

"What's wrong with him?" I heard Gossamer ask Kane, who gave me an odd look, then poked a finger at my forehead. I flinched away from his touch in pain.

"Oh, jeez!" he yelled. "I think he's got a concussion! There's a lump on his head the size of a golf ball!"

*Teleport...Teleport...*I *know* that word...

Gossamer pulled out one of her daggers. "I think I could–"

"No!" Kane told her. "You're too weak!"

Teleport...Teleport... As I tried to concentrate, I glanced at Estrella, who lifted her head to the sky, screamed, and vanished.

"Oh!" I said in sudden realization. "Teleport!"

A second later we were at the Academy, in the room with the vortex gate.

MUTATION

Chapter 38

I have to give Gavin credit; he did an excellent job of rounding everyone up. The room where the vortex normally opened - and the hallway leading into it - was completely packed. It looked like everyone was there, and already wearing their sunglasses.

Magnavolt, despite looking haggard and withdrawn, had taken charge of things since being brought out of sedation just an hour or so earlier. We found him and several of his senior staff near the gate (or rather, what was left of it), trying to keep order. Gavin had already brought him up to speed on everything regarding the virus, and we briefed him on the mission we'd just completed.

"I hate to have to tell you this," he said when we'd finished, "especially after everything you went through, but I think it's a bust."

"Why's that?" asked Kane.

"Because the vortex opened before you got here," Magnavolt said. "It was only for a few seconds – not long enough for anyone to go through. Everyone's been waiting around, hoping it will open again."

"I guess that explains why everyone already has their sunglasses on," I said.

"So, after all that," Gossamer said, "we're still stuck here."

"And in a few minutes almost all of the students here will start losing control of their powers," Kane added.

I didn't have the heart to tell them about the additional danger posed by Estrella, who could possibly go supernova at any moment and fry the whole planet to a cinder. I don't know if anyone else noticed, but I could hear the wind outside starting to build. I felt someone take my hand; I turned and saw Electra standing there, with Smokey behind her. She gave me a kiss.

"You never showed up for dinner," she said with a pout.

I smiled. If this is how things were going to end, I was glad to have the people I cared about at my side. I thought back to Adam's last moments...

All of a sudden there was a brilliant burst of light from the direction of the gate. Anyone who hadn't been looking in that direction turned their head that way now.

A silhouette slowly took shape at the edge of the gate as the vortex opened up. I switched my vision over and almost jumped for joy when I saw who was standing there.

"Anybody need a ride home?" asked Mouse nonchalantly, with the ever-present tablet under his arm.

There was a loud cheer, and people started pressing forward. Magnavolt took to the air, floating in front of the gate, voice booming.

"QUICKLY AND IN ORDERLY FASHION, PEOPLE! THIS IS NOT SOME CATTLE DRIVE!"

Mouse stepped down from the gate as people started to go through the vortex.

"We did it!" Kane screamed. "We did it!"

"I don't know that *we* did anything," Gossamer said. "It looks like this is all work they did on the other side – on Earth."

"Still, I like to think we helped," Kane said.

We all stood back as everyone started to file through. I wanted to talk to Mouse, but he was too busy, first speaking to Magnavolt, then running out of the room to do something else. When he came back in, he looked worried.

I grabbed him by the arm. "What is it? What's happening?"

"Something's going on here," he replied. "I don't know exactly what, but some kind of gravity well is forming on this world and growing fast, becoming more powerful by the second. The vortex is providing some stability for the area we're in, but it won't last. The rest of the school's already coming apart. We've got to move faster, before it sucks this school, us, and everything else down its throat – including the vortex."

I sighed, then gave him (and everyone else standing around) a thirty-second overview about Estrella and what was – theoretically - happening to her.

"Well, I think the theory's being proven," he stated when I finished. "That said, we should have enough time to make it if we hustle – we only need another minute or two." He clapped me on the shoulder. "You guys did good. I'm glad you came through it okay."

"Not all of us," said Gossamer.

For a moment I didn't know what she was talking about, then I remembered.

"Li!" I shouted. "I've got to go back for him!"

Before anyone could protest, I teleported back to the garage.

****

When I popped into Manny's Garage, the wind outside was audibly ferocious and blowing in the direction where we had last seen Estrella. From what I could see out the window, there wasn't another building

241

on the street…or the next street, or the next, and so on. I also didn't see a tree, shrub, bush, or blade of grass…anything. Whatever was happening to Estrella, it was, as Mouse indicated, sucking this entire world dry.

That being the case, I was actually surprised to find the garage still in one piece, but then I remembered what Mouse had just said about the vortex providing stability. Although there was no vortex here, the machinery was still on, and maybe that was enough.

Apparently I was getting ahead of myself, though, because the next second the north end of the building ripped away from its foundation and went soaring off into the distance towards something that looked like a shining white dot. Slightly panicked, I flew up to where the industrial magnet was located. This area, being a bit closer to the vortex machinery, seemed slightly more stable, but I knew it wouldn't last long; the roof was already coming apart.

Li was still there, stuck on the magnet like he'd been welded to it. I spent a minute or two zipping around the garage looking for the magnet's controls. One set of equipment that I thought might control it actually raised a hydraulic lift I hadn't noticed before. Another opened a set of bay doors on the east wall. Finally, knowing time was running out, I gave up on finding the controls and flew up to see if there was anything I could do otherwise.

Looking at Li closely, I could see that he was horribly shredded. Thanks to the magnet, Schaefer had really been able to do a number on him. Almost every part of his interior was exposed and obviously damaged: frayed wires, ripped couplings, busted hydraulics. It didn't look like there was anything to be done even if I could get him off the magnet.

MUTATION

I was about to teleport away when I caught a brief flash of colored light from the area of his sternum. Telekinetically, I peeled back part of the housing that made up his chest and the accompanying wires and connections. There, in the center, I saw the piece of ceramic I had observed earlier when he'd been wounded. Using my telekinesis, I took hold of it and pulled. It seemed to snap right out. I took the ceramic in my hand and teleported back to the school just as the rest of the garage blew away.

MUTATION

Chapter 39

Often, when I teleport to a potentially hostile environment, I make sure to pop up phased so as to avoid injury. In this instance, I thought I knew where I was headed – the Academy's vortex gate – so I didn't bother taking any precautions.

When I appeared, however, I didn't seem to be at the school. In fact, I didn't see *anything* that I recognized, because there didn't seem to be anything there to see except a massive windstorm that was blowing everything away. In essence, the school was gone; my efforts to rescue Li had taken too much time. Even worse, when I arrived, I was immediately and wickedly bonked on the noggin by some piece of metal debris, and at the same time I was savagely swept up into the storm.

I had trouble concentrating and felt blood starting to smear on the side of my face as I was swirled around so fast that I became dizzy and nauseous. I phased, which released me from the grip of the tempest. Now that I was still, I could see that the entire pull of the storm was in one direction: towards the area where Manny's Garage was located. Everything was being sucked towards that area – towards the gravity well Mouse had mentioned. Estrella.

My eyes fluttered, and I felt myself starting to become solid again. I began to get pulled by the storm once more. I shook my head and focused as hard as I could on staying phased, feeling relieved when the wind let me go. Still, my eyelids felt heavy and I was having trouble concentrating. Counting the fight with Estrella, I had just received several significant blows to the head in a very short time frame. If I didn't have a concussion before, I surely had one now, as my inability to think straight attested. I needed to find the vortex *now*, assuming it was still open.

I knew that the storm had dragged me for a while before I phased, so I probably wasn't anywhere near the vortex gate at the moment. In fact, even switching my vision over to other wavelengths, I couldn't find any landmarks that I recognized or reference points that were familiar. The gravity well had pulled away everything but bare ground, and even that was disappearing fast. There wasn't even–

There!

I saw a circular spark of light that seemed familiar off to my right. It was the vortex! It had to be! I started to head towards it and immediately felt sick again. My eyes started fluttering once more, and I felt myself losing the tenuous grip I currently had on my powers.

Mentally, I struggled as hard as I could, focusing everything I had on staying phased and heading towards that light. It was no good; I felt myself slowly succumbing to the dark embrace of unconsciousness. I looked towards the light - the vortex - which was becoming smaller by the second, letting me know that I was substantial again and getting pulled towards the gravity well. I raised my hand to my chest, thankful to see that I still held Li's core processor. This way neither of us would die alone. Then everything went dark.

Chapter 40

For just the second time in my life (not counting the day I was born), I woke up in a hospital room. My mother and grandfather, who were in the room with me, immediately looked in my direction. My mother had bags under her eyes, something I'd never seen before. Moreover, her eyes were completely red, evidence that she had been doing quite a bit of crying.

She rushed over and gave me a hug. Needless to say, she began crying again.

Gramps stood back, presenting a stoic demeanor.

<About time,> he said, mentally. <I'm missing an ex-capes convention because of this nonsense with you.>

I smiled. Despite the comment, I was aware of the deep sense of relief Gramps felt, just like my mother, knowing that I had apparently recovered. As even more evidence of how he felt, he eventually shoved Mom out of the way so he could give me a hug as well.

"How long?" I croaked, my throat dry.

"Four days," Mom said. "You had two massive concussions, various cuts and bruises, radiation poisoning—"

"Radiation poisoning?" I asked incredulously.

"That's what they said," Gramps responded.

For a second I wondered how that could have happened, and then I remembered that stars give off radiation. Therefore, it had to have been Estrella. That also would have explained why I suddenly got nauseous while fighting her (although a concussion can cause that as well.)

"Wait a minute," I said, snapping back to the present. "Where am I?"

"Don't worry," Gramps said. "It's not a regular hospital. It's a place for capes. Any secrets a super has when he comes here stay under wraps."

I sighed in relief. I should have known Gramps and Mom wouldn't let me end up in just any hospital. They were the ones who had always insisted on keeping my unique physiology a secret.

We visited together about an hour, with me insisting that I was fine – aside from being hungry enough to eat a horse. During that time, the doctors and nurses came and checked me out.

"You've made a remarkable recovery," one of the doctors noted. "Your family wouldn't authorize any conventional treatment – just an IV drip and round-the-clock surveillance." He looked at Mom and Gramps as he said this, as if their concept of medical care included bloodletting with leeches.

"But your body seems to have done all the work and healed itself," he continued, "even from the radiation poisoning – we were even able to take all of the bandages off yesterday. Hmmm… I don't suppose you'd consider being part of a study–"

"No," all three of us – me, Mom, and Gramps – said simultaneously.

A short time after the last doctor left – and after I'd finally gotten some food in me – there was a soft knock on my door. I looked up to find Mouse, Electra, and Smokey in the doorway.

"Is he up for visitors yet?" Smokey asked no one in particular.

"Sure," said Mom. "Come on in."

"If we aren't intruding, that is," said Mouse.

"Of course not," said my grandfather. "I've seen enough of his mug for now anyway. Come on, Geneva, let's go get some coffee."

Gramps and Mom left, but not before my mother and Electra gave each other a kiss on the cheek and exchanged pleasantries.

"What was that about?" I asked Electra as she sat down and took my hand.

"What?" she asked.

"You and my mom acting like old girlfriends," I said.

"You didn't know?" asked Mouse. "Those two have practically been tag-team partners in terms of holding a vigil by your bedside."

"Yeah," Smokey agreed. "One of them was always here."

I looked at Electra, but she wouldn't meet my gaze – she just lowered her head, smiling. I thought how lucky it was that she had survived the virus–

"The virus!" I shouted. "What–"

"No worries on that front," Mouse said. "A friend and I were able to come up with a vaccine. Everyone's fine for the most part."

I let out a sigh of relief. But Mouse's statement just brought up a million more questions. Before I could ask them, however, a voice I never wished to hear again sounded from the door.

"Is this a private party or can anyone join?" asked Gray.

I frowned, clenching my fist in anger. "What are you doing here, Gray?"

"That's all I get – 'Gray'?" he asked, walking into the room in his trademark gray suit. He stopped at the foot of my bed. "No 'Mister'? Youth today really have no respect."

I repeated my question. "What are you doing here?"

"I just came to check up on you. After all, you know how interested I am in your welfare."

"All I know is that you sent that maniac Schaefer to the Academy with an agenda to kill us all."

"Mr. Schaefer was attached to a humanitarian mission that went to the Academy to help battle the outbreak of a deadly pathogen."

"No, he went there to *spread* that pathogen, because he hated supers. I heard him admit as much. He said they killed his family."

Gray hesitated a moment. "When he was young, Schaefer was with his family on a boat that capsized. He spent six hours in the water and was being circled by sharks when a super rescued him. They never found his parents, and over time he came to blame supers for not saving them. However, that's a long way from wanting to kill them all."

Gray's statement explained a lot about Schaefer, but not enough to excuse his actions.

"Look, you can't sugarcoat this," I said. "Schaefer went to the Academy to deliberately infect students, and he was happy to kill people in the process, including my friend Adam."

"It's my understanding that your friend Adam Atom went crazy. He killed another student, then broke out of his nullifier containment unit and destroyed a bunch of school property – including the vortex gate – before blowing himself up. He was a maniac and a menace."

"Uh-uh," I said, shaking my head. "Schaefer used the virus to amp up Adam's power. As far as I'm concerned, what he did to Adam was the same as cutting the brake line in someone's car so that they have an accident that kills somebody. Adam didn't kill that student; Schaefer did.

"As to breaking out of that cell he was in, someone turned the nullifier off. Adam blew the locks on his cell door and left because he could feel himself losing control. He was about to go nuclear and he knew it, so he was trying to get as far from the Academy as possible. He saved everyone in that school. He's a hero."

"And how do you know all this?"

"Because I looked into his mind at the end and he told me. He also didn't blow up the vortex gate. That was Schaefer, too."

"My, my, you seem to blame a lot on Mr. Schaefer."

"I blame him a lot because he did a lot. He killed Adam on a whim, not because Adam had ever done anything to him, but because he was my friend. That's your lapdog Schaefer. So believe me when I say that he's dead, I'm glad he's dead, and I'm happier that he's dead because of me!"

That last wasn't exactly true, but I didn't mind taking credit for it. However, Mouse, Electra, and Smokey all went bug-eyed at the statement.

Gray just clucked his tongue and came around to my bedside, smiling. He reached into a pocket and pulled out a pair of handcuffs. He slapped one cuff on my wrist and the other to one of the side rails of my hospital bed.

"What's that about?" asked Mouse.

"Your friend here just admitted to killing a federal agent. I already had a warrant to take him into custody, but now I get to arrest him for murder. I need to make sure he stays put until the doctor says he can leave." He turned and started to leave, whistling.

"Hey, Gray," I said. He turned back towards me. I teleported the cuffs off my wrist and the handrail, then flung them at him telekinetically. He flinched a little as they hit him in the chest, but he caught them as they dropped.

"You won't need the cuffs," I said. "I'll be where you can find me."

He frowned a little at that, then turned and left the room, closing the door behind him. Almost immediately Mouse turned to Electra and Smokey.

"Guys, can you give me and Jim a moment?" he asked.

Smokey and Electra nodded and left the room, whispering in hushed tones about what had transpired between me and Gray.

"Is there some special school where they teach you how to make any given situation worse?" Mouse asked when we were alone. "Because the flair you have for it goes far beyond any natural ability."

"Sorry," I said, "but that guy just rubs me the wrong way."

"Is it true about Schaefer? Did you kill him?"

"Not exactly." I explained what happened.

"Well," Mouse said when I finished, "let's make sure you tell it that way when you make your official statement – if it comes to that." That last part made me feel that he had something in mind, but I asked another question instead.

"How'd I get back through the vortex?" I asked. "The last thing I remember is trying to get to it, but I know I didn't make it."

"Alpha Prime," he said plainly. "That place started coming apart even faster than I predicted. We couldn't wait for you on that side any longer, but we kept the vortex tunnel open, hoping you'd come through. We were getting ready to shut it down - it would have sucked the entire Earth through - when Alpha Prime came bursting in."

"I guess it can't be an amazing rescue unless the world's greatest superhero is involved," I said with derision.

"No, that's not it at all. Once he heard you were on the other side, we couldn't stop him. I even told him not to go, that he'd probably be killed if he did."

I sat up. "What? I didn't think anything could kill Alpha Prime."

"I didn't know if it could or couldn't, but you have to understand something. From what you told me, it sounded like Estrella was going through the life cycle of a star in record time. Red giant, white dwarf…"

Red giant!

He trailed off in confusion as I started laughing, so I had to tell him about Estrella *literally* becoming a red giant.

"Interesting," he said. "That's exactly what happens to a star – it becomes massively huge and red. Hence the name red giant. But at the time I arrived, I think she was in the white dwarf stage of the life cycle…"

As Mouse explained it, the gravity of a white dwarf is about 100,000 times that of Earth. After that, the star explodes, going supernova.

252

"And at some juncture after that," Mouse said, "a black hole forms, with gravity so strong that not even light can escape."

"And if we'd been stuck on the other side," I said, "we would have had to go through all that."

"Now you see why I say he might not have survived. In all honesty, I didn't think he'd even be able to escape the gravitational pull of the white dwarf, and I told him as much."

"But he came anyway." I suddenly had a newfound respect for my father.

"As I said, once he heard you were still over there, there was no stopping him. And somehow – against all odds – he found you and brought you back. He saved your life."

At that point, a nurse came and announced that visiting hours were over. Everyone came around once more to say their goodbyes, and then I was alone with my thoughts.

Chapter 41

I slept fitfully that night, awakening a few times with the temptation to just teleport home. If I left without a green light from the doctors, though, Mom would worry, and she'd had enough on her mind lately.

When I woke up the next morning, I felt almost like my old self – despite a restless night. Electra came by shortly after I finished breakfast. We chatted amiably for a while, holding hands, but I could sense a tension building up in her, a need for something. Finally, she asked her question.

"When you got back," she said, "from being with Adam, I mean, why didn't you come see me?"

"You mean to let you know I was alive?" I asked.

"No," she said, shaking her head, "I knew you were alive. I could sense your bioelectric field – at least once you were back at the school."

I was a little surprised. "I didn't know you could extend it that far. I always had the impression that the person had to be in close proximity to you - something like the same room."

"Doesn't have to be *that* close. Still, I never tried reaching out that far before, but I needed to know. Anyway, maybe I just pushed myself or maybe it was the virus, but I knew when you were back on campus. But you didn't come see me."

I explained Li's theory about how seeing me might trigger the virus, so I had kept my distance. She nodded, seeming to understand.

"Plus," I added, "you were under quarantine."

She laughed, giving me a playful punch. "You know what the worst part of quarantine was?"

"Missing me?"

"The food!" she exclaimed, ignoring me. "They issued us seven days' worth of meals-ready-to-eat!"

"MREs?"

"Yes, and they were awful! I'd rather eat a pot full of dirt. Too bad your friend Li didn't have a theory on how to get us some real food, but at least we didn't have to eat the entire week's supply of them."

The mention of Li put me in mind of my other friends, so I asked about Kane and Gossamer.

"Oh, no one told you," Electra said. "They're here. They even checked in on you a few times."

With a little bit of coaxing, one of the nurses told us what rooms Kane and Gossamer were in. Both were in the same wing, one floor up.

We took the stairs and tried Kane's room first. It was empty. We decided to try Gossamer's next, but long before we reached her door we heard arguing drifting out from the room. I grinned, suddenly having a very good notion of where Kane was.

Sure enough, he was in Gossamer's room. She had her bed in an upright position and he was sitting on the edge of it, next to her. Gossamer had an impressive amount of gauze wrapped around her head, all intended to keep a bandage in place over her right eye. Kane had bandages wrapped around his wrists. (It turned out that Estrella had given him third-degree burns.) The two of them were currently engaged in heated debate, but that stopped abruptly when I knocked.

"Hey," Gossamer said, "I heard you were up."

I went inside and gave her a hug, then gently shook Kane's hand before taking a seat in a nearby chair.

I started to introduce Electra, who stood next to my chair, but the three of them already knew each other.

"How's the eye?" I asked Gossamer.

"Pretty much blind at the moment," she said, in better spirits than I would have imagined. "Hopefully it won't stay that way."

"I feel so bad," Electra said. "The things you guys had to do to save the rest of us."

Kane gave her a mockingly smug grin. "All in a day's work, my dear."

We chatted about everything that had happened for another half hour, at which point Electra and I made to leave. As we were walking out, I heard Gossamer and Kane go right back to arguing about apparently the same subject they were discussing when we arrived.

I turned back to them. "Hey, Kane. Why don't you just kiss her?"

"W-What?" Kane sputtered, almost in shock. "Kiss her? I'd rather kiss a dead—"

His words were cut off when Gossamer, taking the initiative, grabbed him by his shirt and pulled his lips to hers. I couldn't help but notice that, despite the protest he was just making, he didn't pull away. Electra and I closed the door behind us as we left.

****

Walking back to my hospital room, I couldn't help smiling again as I thought of Gossamer and Kane finally being a couple. Theirs had been an odd courtship, but who was I to talk? My first date with Electra had ended up with her blasting me with a bolt of electricity.

As we got closer to the room, I could hear voices raised in argument. Unlike the banter between Gossamer and Kane, however, there was real anger behind the words being spoken.

The door to my room was partly open. Electra and I crept up and peeked through the crack where the hinges of the door were located, her bending down below me.

Gray and some of the MIBs were in the room, as were Mouse, Mom, and Gramps.

"-ibly be real," Gray said, looking at some papers in his hand. "You manufactured this."

"Oh, it's real," said Mouse. "Prince J'h'dgo is a member of the royal house – the royal family, in fact – and is therefore entitled to everything written in that charter."

"Who the heck is Prince Jargo?" Electra whispered, mangling the name.

I gulped. "I think it's me." I felt more than saw Electra's face swivel up towards me. I'd heard the pronunciation of my name in my alien grandmother's language even less often than I'd heard my full name in English. And as for being a prince, I guess it was something I always knew was technically true, but I'd never lived any kind of regal lifestyle. To have the title suddenly applied to me seemed surreal.

"In short," Mouse said, "he's a prince, a dignitary and a diplomat, and that charter gives him full immunity. Moreover, it's retroactive, covering anything he's done in the past. You can't touch him."

Gray grunted angrily and headed towards the door. Electra and I hugged the wall as he stormed out and down the hallway, followed by his subordinates. We then slipped into the room.

Mom, grinning widely, came over and gave me a big hug and a kiss on the cheek.

"I don't think we'll be having any more issues with Gray," Gramps said. "At least not officially."

"Why's that?" I asked. "What happened?"

"Gray seems to have forgotten that when your grandmother came to this planet, it was as the envoy and emissary of a foreign government," Mouse said. "She was granted full diplomatic status – as was her family – including diplomatic immunity."

"And the diplomatic charter was never rescinded," Gramps added. "It was inactive for a while, but never revoked. So we just filed the paperwork establishing the installation of a new ambassador, and that reactivated the charter."

"So," I said, working it all out in my mind, "I have diplomatic immunity?"

"Yes!" said Mom excitedly, almost clapping her hands. "They can't arrest you for any crime you committed!"

"Can we say, 'Allegedly committed'?" I asked. "But still, that's pretty cool!"

Mouse got the attention of Mom and Gramps to discuss something else, and Electra took the opportunity to have a whispered conversation with me.

"So," she said in a low voice, "I'm the girlfriend of a prince?"

"Oh," I replied in mock indignation, "now that I'm a prince, you're my girlfriend? Well, no thank you; I see no need to settle or start dating down."

She gave me a playful punch on the arm, then spent a few seconds tickling me.

"By the way, who's the new ambassador?" I asked no one in particular after Electra stopped her playful assault on me.

The silence in the room was deafening as all three adults turned to look at me.

Oh no...

Chapter 42

I was dismissed from the hospital the next morning. After letting Mom fuss over me for an hour or so after arriving home, I decided it was time to start getting the answers to some questions I'd been curious about. With that in mind, I called Mouse and asked when would be a good time for me to drop by his lab. He said any time, and I was standing next to him before he could put the phone down.

"How'd I know that was going to happen the second I said those words?" Mouse asked. He was sitting at a worktable, looking at some schematics.

I just smiled, glancing around the lab. There were banks of sophisticated computers and machinery along one wall. A set of bookshelves hid the entrance to a secret chamber. At least a dozen flat screen monitors placed strategically around the lab constantly displayed a steady stream of information. It was just like the last time I'd been here.

"Okay," Mouse said, "what do you want to know?"

"For starters, how is it all the students managed to be okay?" I asked. "Even without the control module Schaefer had, my friend Li said that the virus would unravel their DNA in just a couple of days."

"We were able to develop a vaccine. We gave it to them once they all came through. In fact, we're giving it to every meta on the planet."

"A vaccine? How'd you develop a vaccine? How'd you even know about the virus in the first place?"

"With this," Mouse said. He opened up a drawer at his worktable and took out a cylindrical item, which he laid in front of him. It was a syringe.

"What's that? I mean, I know it's a syringe, but what's the significance of it?"

"Well, I'm just sitting here minding my own business one day, when all of a sudden *this* thing pops up next to me. I'm curious, so I go test the liquid inside and find that it's actually got some of your blood in it. *Infected* blood."

Unexpectedly, I had a flashback of Dr. Prasad telling me how they tried to inject me with something and that I teleported the syringe. I also remember the weird dream I had with the mouse and the snake. Somehow, I had managed to teleport something across dimensions! The thought of it was almost enough to completely freak me out.

"Wait," I said. "How'd you know it was *my* blood?"

"I didn't initially, but I had enough clues. There was the fact that it had obviously been teleported here - and teleporters are rare - the strange anomalies in the blood, and a couple of other things. I was sure, but I called BT for confirmation, which she provided."

That made sense. BT was the closest thing to a medical professional I had ever let come near me – before recently, that is – and she would know my blood at a glance.

"Don't be mad at BT," Mouse said. "I know you might feel she betrayed your trust in confirming your blood, but she did what she thought was in your best interest."

I shook my head. "I'm not mad; it was the right call. She saved a lot of lives."

"I'm glad you see it that way."

"What about the vortex? Your timing couldn't have been better if we'd planned it."

"The minute we found out it was your blood, we tried to conference with the Academy and couldn't get through. That's not completely unusual. It was in a different dimension, after all - not like making a call to a neighbor down the street. But when we couldn't get through after a day or so, we decided to open the vortex."

"And?"

"Since our equipment isn't designed to punch all the way through anymore, from one dimension to another, we were hoping someone on the other side would see that we were trying to get through and open their end of the vortex. When that didn't happen, we had to reconfigure our equipment to do things the old-fashioned way - not to mention getting a special dispensation to re-route a tremendous amount of power. It took a little bit of time."

I absorbed all of this in silence, and then something occurred to me.

"That special dispensation...did that come from the government?" I asked.

"Of course."

"That was the tip-off," I said. "That's why they tried to abort everything so fast. They knew you were coming."

Mouse seemed to consider this. "Possibly. Gray's got his hand in almost every cookie jar imaginable, so they could have gotten a heads-up. But even so, we still almost bungled the whole thing."

"What do you mean?"

"We actually needed two bites at the apple to get things right. We were doing everything in such a rush that we didn't notice that our dimensional alignment was off, so when we first opened the vortex, it actually didn't take us to the Academy. We ended up on the top of some mountain range.

"We were about to shut everything down and re-run all the numbers when we detected a brief vortex pulse."

"Our attempt to open the vortex from our side," I said, guessing.

"Yes. It didn't work, but it showed us where our calculations were off, so we reset everything based on the new numbers and that did it."

I smiled to myself, thinking how Li - despite not being able to open the vortex as we'd planned - had still been instrumental in saving everyone. That brought something else to mind.

"Were you there when Alpha Prime came back through the vortex with me?" I asked.

"I was the first one to meet him," Mouse said.

"Before I lost consciousness on the other side," I said, "before AP found me, I'd been holding a piece of ceramic. Do you know if I still had it when we came back through?"

"Oh, yes," Mouse said, smiling. "You had a death grip on that thing, so tight that I thought we'd have to break your fingers to get it loose. It's a wonder you didn't crush it."

"Do you know what happened to it?"

"I don't know," Mouse said, grinning. "Let me think…"

He got up from the worktable and walked over to an odd piece of computer equipment and flipped a small switch.

"Hello," he said, looking up into the air, but at nothing in particular. "Can you hear us?"

"I can," said a voice that - although disembodied - I had no trouble recognizing.

"Li!" I said, totally shocked. "You're alive!"

"Technically," said the voice, which seemed to come from all around us, "I was never alive biologically, but I am still functional."

"It's good to hear your voice," I said with a smile.

"Yours, too," said Li. "Unfortunately, while I have audio receptors and a voice module, visual sensory has not yet been established."

"I'm working on it," Mouse said in mock anger, holding up the schematics he'd been looking at. Now that I looked more closely, I could see that they were designs for an android.

Noting my interest, Mouse handed me one of the drawings. "I'm working on building Li a new body," he said. "It would be great if I could consult with his designer, but he doesn't know who built him."

That brought a whole new series of questions to mind, but I decided to leave those for another time. Instead I asked, "How'd you even know what he was?"

"When I finally was able to pry it away from you," Mouse said, "I could tell that what you were holding was some kind of processor. I hooked it into one of my machines to see what I could find out about it, and Li started communicating with me. It didn't take long to figure out that I was dealing with an artificial intelligence."

MUTATION

All of a sudden, I felt bad for intruding. Mouse was here trying to do something important, and I'd selfishly come barging in because I thought my own need for answers took priority over anything else. I mentioned to Li that Kane and Gossamer were more than okay, and prepared to leave.

"Before you go," Mouse said, "I just want to say that you and your friends did an amazing job - but you especially. I think everyone pretty much realizes that if you hadn't been there, we'd be dealing with a lot of bodies right now - especially if Schaefer had brought that virus back to Earth. And even if he didn't kill every super outright, having the virus - and the cure - would have let Schaefer, and presumably Gray, control anyone who was infected."

His words brought to mind Rudi's earlier prediction (Rudi, whom I would still need to rescue whenever I got the requisite info), about how it was imperative that I go to the Academy. I felt a little pompous acknowledging it - even if only to myself - but apparently she had been right.

"What about Gavin?" I asked. "What will happen to him?"

Mouse shrugged. "Hard to say at this point. He was instrumental in spreading the virus at the Academy, but he also came around in the end. Bearing in mind that he's a minor and that there were extenuating circumstances, my best guess is some type of probation."

"I guess that would temper justice with mercy. Anyway, I should let you get back to work," I said to Mouse. "I'll see you later, Li," I just shouted up into the air.

"Jim," Li said, almost timidly, as I was preparing to teleport. "It may be a while before my new body is manufactured. In the meantime, will you…will you come visit me sometimes?"

"Of course, Li. I'll bring the others, too, if that's okay."

****

There was only one other person I really needed to talk to, and it was a conversation I both looked forward to and dreaded. Still, I made the call, and he showed up right on time.

Mom and Gramps had found reasons to be somewhere else, so there was no one else at home when Alpha Prime showed up. He was wearing a V-neck sweater-shirt and jeans; it was far more casual than I'd ever even pictured him, let alone seen him. We went into the kitchen and took seats around the breakfast table.

"Thanks for inviting me over," he said. "The invitation was unexpected, but I'm happy about it."

"No problem," I said. "I, uh, I would have been happy to come to you, but I don't know where you live. Other than League facilities, that is."

He laughed at that. "I'm sorry, I should have told you. But yes, I have a place - several places, in fact. I just need to get away sometimes."

I nodded, picking up a slight hint of exhaustion in his voice. He'd mentioned it to me before, about how having to deal with all the world's-greatest-superhero stuff just felt like an unbearable weight sometimes.

"Anyway," I said, "I just wanted to say thanks for what you did. They told me how you came after me. You saved my life."

He waved off my gratitude. "You don't have to thank me for that. Not now; not ever. You're my son, so it's not like I had a choice. It was either get to you or die trying."

There was an earnestness to his words that touched me. He wasn't saying any of this to make me like him or think highly of him. He was saying it because it was true.

"The last time we spoke," I said, "you mentioned something about sons needing their fathers. I didn't agree with you then, but I do now. Not because you saved my life, but because of the example you set. That's probably the greatest need that fathers fulfill for their sons - a role model. And according to Mouse, I need all the role models I can get."

"Thanks," he said, before adding almost furtively, "son."

"Anyway, since the Academy is destroyed now and I'm back home permanently, there's no need to wait for the holidays to go catch that game."

For a second, he didn't seem to know what I was talking about, and then he grinned. "I can get courtside tickets for next week."

THE END

Manufactured by Amazon.ca
Bolton, ON